Ju
F
C81   Corcoran, Barbara.
            The clown.

DATE	ISSUED TO
JAN '66	

Ju
F   Corcoran, Barbara.
C81   The clown.

Temple Israel Library
Minneapolis, Minn.

Please sign your full name on the above card.

Return books promptly to the Library or Temple Office.

Fines will be charged for overdue books or for damage or loss of same.

the Clown

the Clown

BARBARA CORCORAN

Atheneum   1975   New York

I wish to thank the office of the
Danish Embassy in London for information
about the procedures used with defectors.

Copyright © 1975 by Barbara Cocoran
All rights reserved
Published simultaneously in Canada by
McClelland & Stewart Ltd.
Manufactured in the United States of America
Printed by Sentry Press, New York
Bound by The Book Press, Inc.
Brattleboro, Vermont
First Edition

"I Wish You Love" (Que Reste-t-il Nos Amours?)
English Lyric by Albert A. Beach
French Lyric and Music by Charles Trenet
© Copyright 1946, 1955, 1956 by Editions Salabert, France
Leeds Music Corporation, 445 Park Avenue, New York, N.Y. 10022
Sole selling Agent for the USA and Canada
Used by permission
All rights reserved

LIBRARY OF CONGRESS CATALOGING IN PUBLICATION DATA

Corcoran, Barabara.   The clown.
SUMMARY: A sixteen-year-old American girl becomes
involved with a circus clown in Moscow who is
sought after by the KGB.   [1. Escapes—Fiction]
[2. Russia—Fiction. 3. Copenhagen—Fiction] I. Title.
PZ7.C814Cl   [Fic]   75-8759   ISBN 0-689-30465-X

to Lynn Bowers

1

Liza cracked the shell of the hard-boiled egg that she had brought to her room from the hotel buffet. She ate the egg slowly, looking out the window at Moscow. Below her, very close, was the golden onion dome of a little brick chapel, the gilt crosses on its four smaller dark-green domes gleaming in the gray light of a rainy afternoon. The workmen had been restoring it when she was here with her father almost a year ago. If she leaned out, she could see some of the other chapels: the two that were apricot-colored and white, the pale blue one. Her father had said that Ivan the Terrible had had them built in fits of remorse after some of his especially wicked deeds.

From here she couldn't see the Cathedral of St. Basil

the Beatified, but she thought how astounded she had been when she first saw it, all those spires and minarets and the astonishing colors. There were eight pillars built around a big central pillar, all of them different-colored with domes bulging at the top. It was like something a child might make out of Play-Doh after he'd read the *Arabian Nights*. In fact, all of Moscow seemed to her like a fantasy—ancient churches and palaces all mixed up with ultramodern buildings. It was such a shock to the senses it had made her laugh with surprise.

She and her father had come for a quick vacation last year before he took up his new assignment at the consulate in Copenhagen. He had wanted for a long time to be posted to Copenhagen, and he was happy.

She gathered up the pieces of eggshell and dumped them in the trash basket. Aunt May and Uncle George were downstairs, in the dining room for independent tourists. Uncle George had had the idea that if you went early you might get a table. It wouldn't work. You'd just get *"niet, niet,"* and you'd be shooed away like mosquitoes. When she was here with her father, they'd either eaten at friends' apartments, people from the embassy that her father knew, or they went with them to the Aragvi or somewhere. There were never any problems when she traveled with her father.

She leaned her cheek against the cool windowpane. Two blocks away the five ruby-red stars of the Kremlin would be glowing and revolving, but the only one she could see was the one on top of the bell tower of Ivan the Great.

Uncle George had tried to get Liza to ring up her

4

father's friends so he could get introductions, but she wouldn't do it. She wasn't going to use her father that way. Uncle George was a professional photographer, not very successful mainly because he went about everything the wrong way. Some publisher he knew had mentioned he'd like to do a picture book, a "coffee-table book," on the Russian theater, so Uncle George had rushed off on this trip, without even a commitment. That was the way he did things. He would quibble and fuss over getting his money's worth at lunch or over a tip, but then he'd blow a lot of money on a trip like this, with no guarantee at all.

He had written to the Minister of Culture and to the directors of the Bolshoi and the Moscow Art Theater, and he had expected them to answer right away, welcoming him to take pictures; but of course they hadn't written at all. Everybody—except Uncle George—knew that bureaucrats moved slowly, and Russian bureaucrats the slowest of all. Poor Uncle George. She was glad he was not her real uncle, only the husband of her mother's half sister.

When Aunt May paid for a transatlantic call, just before Liza's school year ended, to invite her on a trip to Moscow, Liza knew they must want something. She had only come because she wanted to see Moscow again, no matter how much it hurt. She wanted to recapture some of that trip with her father. She had heard the relief in Aunt May's voice when she had said she would pay her own way. And as soon as they got here, she realized they had brought her because they thought she would get Uncle George introduced to the right people, so he could take his pictures. She had not done it.

5

"You'd think," Uncle George kept saying, "with a brother-in-law that spent his life in the consular service, I'd get some respect."

Liza was left free to roam around back streets and walk along the bank of the river while they trailed along behind the Intourist guide, seeing the sights.

She heard the key in the door of the room next to hers, Aunt May's and Uncle George's room, and then she heard their voices. She got the water glass from the bathroom and held it to the wall, the other end of the glass against her ear. She reached out and switched off the lamp on the desk so she was in shadow. She had heard that the rooms in the newer tourist hotels were not only bugged but wired for closed-circuit television. Although she wasn't sure why she cared, she didn't want those people on the twenty-first floor watching her while she eavesdropped on her relatives.

Uncle George was easier to hear than Aunt May. He was fuming about being pushed around by the waitresses and finally having to give two vouchers apiece for their dinner.

"If I see another bowl of borsch," he said, "I'll throw it at them. Cabbages! The damned country is awash in cabbages!"

"Hush," Aunt May said. "They're listening."

"Oh, God," he said in a lower voice. "I forgot."

"You always forget."

Although he spoke more quietly, Liza could hear him plainly. He must have been just on the other side of the wall. "Between remembering that stuff and re- membering what dopes we were to drag along that niece of yours, a man could go nutty."

"Liza isn't any bother to you," Aunt May said.

"Nor any help."

"Well, it seemed like a good idea at the time." There was a mumble that Liza couldn't hear. Then more clearly: "She's nothing like her mother. Ethel was so outgoing and warm. Poor Ethel."

"Let's don't start weeping over your sister," Uncle George said. "She's been dead six years."

"You're a heartless monster," Aunt May said, but she didn't sound angry.

"I never liked your sister."

"Nobody asked you to."

"Don't like any of your family. You'd better put in a call to your old man, by the way."

"You don't like my family, but you like their money."

"May, money makes the mare go. I don't pretend. We need money. If your father dies and you aren't there, it'd be just like your brother to get away with everything. He's probably got him to change his will by now, on the basis that you wouldn't go skylarking off to Russia when he had a heart attack if you really cared about him. I can just hear it."

"I wouldn't have come if I'd known Father was going to be so sick."

"Neither would I, believe me."

"But I mean, because he's my father, not just because of the money."

"Be practical. You know it's the money. You were never buddies."

"George, sometimes you make me sick."

"I know, dear. Where's my blue-and-white shirt?"

"Right in front of you."

7

There was no talk for a couple of minutes. Then Uncle George said, "Is the kid going to the circus with us?"

"Unless she's changed her mind."

"That would be all right by me."

"Well, it is handy when she goes along. She does speak the language, after all. You can never make taxi drivers or anybody understand you."

"They do it on purpose. They hate us. I suppose she won't say a word all evening. Lord, I can't stand kids. What are they thinking about anyway? She stares at me with those big gray eyes like I'm a bug under a microscope."

Liza grinned and moved the glass to a better position.

"Have a heart, George. The kid's had a rough time."

"We all have a rough time. At least she could be a little help. You told me she knew people."

"She does. Her father did anyway."

"Fat lot of good it does me. If I don't get some pictures and sell this book, we'll be up a creek, money-wise."

Aunt May sounded depressed. "It's the story of our lives."

"Oh, you don't have such a hard lot." There was a long pause. "Not that necktie. The blue one. I wish I had half the dough that kid has."

"It's her father's side. The Virginia people."

"What does a kid need with a lot of money?"

"Don't get any ideas, George. You'll just bungle it."

A knock on Liza's door made her jump. She dropped the glass and it shattered. As she stooped down to pick up the pieces, Irina, the maid, came in. Irina was small, and she scuttled about in a perpetual flutter that reminded Liza of Mrs. Tittlemouse in the Beatrix Potter books. At the age of thirty-seven or eight, Irina already seemed like a babushka. Liza was one of her special interests. Irina thought she was left too much alone.

She came toward Liza with her quick scurrying steps, her hands under her apron fluttering it up and down. In Russian she said, "Oh, child, what has happened? Did you cut yourself?"

And Liza answered in her own halting Russian. "No. I dropped the glass."

Irina waved her aside, and cleaned up the broken glass. "I must take them the pieces."

Liza knew about that. She had broken a glass when she was here before. The maid was required to produce the broken glass before another one could be issued, and the tourist who broke it had to pay thirty kopeks. Irina didn't want to take Liza's money. Liza wasn't sure what she said, but it had something to do with "arranging things." However, Liza insisted. She didn't want Irina getting into trouble.

"You had dinner?" Irina asked, peering suspiciously at the eggshell in the trash basket.

Liza shrugged. "Enough."

Irina muttered something, casting disapproving glances toward the next room. "A child must eat," she said.

"I'm splendid, Irina, really." And to change the subject she said, "We're going to the circus."

"Ah, the circus! Very good!" Irina was happy that Liza was going to the circus. That was what a child should do. She hugged Liza and hustled off with the little pile of broken glass. Liza smiled. She liked Irina.

Busy as she was, Irina had taken Liza's laundry, washed it and ironed it beautifully, refusing any pay. It was nice when people did things for you just because they liked you or just because they were kind. It didn't happen too often.

When she was dressed for the circus, Liza sat down to read for the third or fourth time the copy of *Persuasion* that her father had given her just before he went to Washington for what was to have been a few days of briefing. On the second day he was shot to death by a thief who was so incompetent that he overlooked four one-hundred-dollar bills in an inside jacket pocket. The man had been caught and sentenced to life imprisonment. Liza thought he should have been executed. Whenever she thought of him, she saw in her mind a man with no face. He had had a stocking over his head during the attack, and she could never picture him with any face at all. At the trial he had said he hadn't intended to kill his victim but he had had to defend himself because the victim had hit him. Liza didn't believe that. Her father was a diplomat by nature and training. He didn't deal with things by hitting people. And he had more sense than to risk his life for a few hundred dollars. The judge didn't believe the man either. Wanton disregard for human life, he had said.

Once Liza had dreamed of challenging the man to a duel. In her dream, the duel took place under big elms along a river. She shot the faceless man where his eyes should have been, and he died instantly; and she felt disappointed because now he was gone and there was nothing more she could do to him. She had told Mademoiselle Bernet about the dream, because it occurred while she was at school. Mademoiselle Bernet, who was her best friend, had had a long talk with her about revenge. When you take revenge, she had said, the person you hurt most is yourself. Liza had thought about that a good deal since. She usually accepted or seriously considered what Mademoiselle Bernet said, but she wasn't sure she was right this time. As far as she knew, Mademoiselle had never personally experienced a desire for revenge, and you couldn't be absolutely sure how things were until you'd experienced them. Even then, sometimes your memory tripped you up.

Mademoiselle said she must stop living in the past and make a new life for herself, but that was easier said than done. She didn't know what a new life would be like. It couldn't be as nice as the old one with her father. Sometimes she tried to pretend that he had not died at all, that he was just away on one of his trips. But it never worked, really.

She tried to remember Mademoiselle's face, but even that familiar face had blurred. It was frightening the way things slipped away. When she had first gone to school in Zurich, at least half the girls in Liza's form had had a crush on Mademoiselle. Not wishing to be identified with such foolishness, Liza had kept her feelings to herself, and for a long time she was so aloof Mademoiselle finally asked her why she disliked her.

Liza remembered that afternoon very well. She had been asked to tea in Mademoiselle's suite. Outside the windows huge snowflakes drifted down and the whole world seemed to have grown silent, outside of time.

"I don't dislike you," she had said, putting sugar in her tea. "Next to my father, I love you more than any-

11

one in the world. But I don't approve of all that mushing about. May I have the cream, please?"

Mademoiselle's gray eyes had widened and then filled with laughter, but all she had said was, "It's fresh cream, just in from the country. I don't care much for mushing about either. I think we shall be good friends."

And they had been, ever since. But on holidays Mademoiselle seemed so far away, almost as if she, too, had died.

Liza had several friends whom she liked, but the only other people she loved were Harriet and Walter Johnson, the couple from Virginia, childhood friends of her father, whom he had asked to be his housekeepers after Liza's mother died. They had had a general store at home, but it had gone broke. Harriet and Walter had stayed on in the Copenhagen apartment after Liza's father was killed. They were her comfort and her home. She hardly remembered her mother except as an invalid, often in great pain, who tried so valiantly to pretend she was all right that her very courage made a gulf Liza couldn't cross. One thing she did know was that her mother was nothing like her half sister May. They had had the same mother, but this father of May's, who was now so ill, was a man Liza had never even met.

When Aunt May and Uncle George finally came to take her to the circus, Uncle George kept hurrying her, as if it were she who had kept them waiting. She took her time putting on her mackintosh, giving her long brown hair one last combing.

It was she, of course, who got the taxi, and she who told the driver where they were going. He grinned at her inexpert Russian, but he understood her. She sat in front with him and nodded and exclaimed politely as he pointed out landmarks that were already familiar. It was beginning to rain, a light silvery rain that made the five red stars of the Kremlin look as if they hung in the sky without earthly support. Liza told the driver she loved the long, ancient-looking wall of the Kremlin, and he beamed. "Fifteenth century," he told her proudly.

When he left them at the big, imposing Moscow Circus, she paid and tipped him while Uncle George was still trying to sort out his Russian currency and muttering to Aunt May about whether he should tip or not. The only thing he was willing to take on faith in the Intourist brochure was that it was not necessary to tip.

They had good seats on one of the center aisles, five rows from the ring. As in all Russian circuses, there was only one ring, and by the time they reached their seats the parade of the performers had already begun. Uncle George was annoyed to find that it was a provincial circus, not the Moscow. It was a circus from Georgia.

"And what good is that to me?" he said angrily, across Liza, who sat between him and Aunt May. "I can't use pictures of some lousy outfit from the sticks, even if I can get them to let me take any."

Aunt May frowned and shushed him, but he muttered for some minutes, studying the program he couldn't read, shifting restlessly in his seat. His thin, pale hair, which was receding at a rate that alarmed him, was plastered to his head by the rain; and his light-blue eyes blinked rapidly as he watched the performers prance around the arena.

Liza went to the Copenhagen Circus often, near the

Tivoli Gardens. Going to the circus was like going to see an old friend. She squirmed contentedly inside her raincoat and forgot about Uncle George. She had loved the Moscow Circus last year, especially Popov, the great clown. This circus was much more informal—almost, it seemed, improvised at times, although she knew that was an illusion. Her father had taken her to a practice session at the Moscow Circus School, where many Soviet circus people were trained from the age of ten or eleven. She had seen how rigorous the training was and how hard they worked.

But now these Georgians, who looked so different from the Muscovites, and who were so dark and slender and full of enthusiasm, walked the high wire, danced on it, did incredible tricks on it, as if it were as easy as skipping across the grass. She had never been to Georgia, but it had been her father's favorite part of Russia.

When the act was finished, Liza joined the audience in the rhythmic clapping to the beat of the band, which meant they approved. She tried to get what the master of ceremonies said, but the amplifiers made him hard for her to understand. She watched the nimble young men who cleared away the paraphernalia of the last act. In Russian circuses the performers took turns acting as crew. She waited expectantly for the next act.

Five beautiful white horses with elegant gold trappings cantered into the ring, heads arched, hooves lifted high. And then the crowd roared with laughter as the sixth horse, a small dappled gray with a wreath of huge artificial sunflowers around his neck, followed the others.

"Oh, what a sweet pony!" Aunt May said, and for a moment Liza felt quite fond of her.

A young woman in a dazzling tunic, satin tights, and white riding boots cracked a whip in the center of the ring. The horses stopped, each putting his front feet on the hindquarters of the horse in front of him. The little gray missed the first time and had to try again. The audience was charmed. All through the act, whatever the white horses did the gray did slightly wrong or a little late. When the young woman finally took her bow, she got a long burst of applause.

Just as the little gray left the ring, trailing his proud white friends, two clowns came in from the other side. One of them was small, not more than five feet tall. The other was tall and thin, with long loosely hung arms and legs. The little one wore baggy pants with big polka dots and a turtleneck sweater. He had a small visored cap that he kept taking off and putting on, sometimes backward or sideways. The tall clown, who looked quite young, wore trousers too short for him, exposing bright purple socks, and he wore a tall stovepipe hat. Except for spots of rouge on each cheek, he had no makeup, but a large pair of glasses kept slipping down his nose. At first the two galloped around the ring, imitating the horse act, the little one taking the part of the little gray horse.

Uncle George leaned toward Aunt May. "I hate clowns," he said.

A huge man in front of them, who had an arm around each of two young children, turned and glared. Then he went back to his enjoyment of the clowns, laughing uproariously and hugging the children. Liza wondered if he understood English or had just been annoyed by Uncle George's tone.

When the clowns came back the second time, after the lion act, they had a new routine. The little one would point his finger at the audience, as a searchlight also moved over the spectators. When he stopped moving his finger and jumped up and down, the searchlight stopped, fixed on someone in the crowd. Then the tall clown whipped out a big sketchpad and with very quick strokes drew a large caricature of the person on whom the light had stopped. He held the sketch up for the audience to see, ran up the steps to the subject of the drawing, and presented it to him, while the crowd clapped.

After he had done this twice on the other side of the ring, the light came sweeping over the area where Liza sat. It hovered, hesitated, moved, jerked back, while people waited in suspense. It lit up Liza, moved to Aunt May, to the big man in front of Liza, and then to Uncle George . . . and it stopped.

Uncle George exclaimed in alarm and shrank back in his seat, but he couldn't escape the relentless light. Already the tall clown was sketching. The people sitting around them called encouragement to Uncle George, who tried to smile but looked like a scared rabbit.

The clown held up the finished sketch. It was Uncle George all right, thin blond hair flat to his head, receding hairline, glasses, flat nose, and look of fright. The crowd laughed and applauded. The clown bounded up the steps, doffed his hat with a bow, and presented the sketch to Uncle George. Uncle George took it without looking at it, trying hard to smile.

The clown looked past him at Liza. He met her eyes with such directness she felt as if there were some electric current between them. His eyes were dark, and he looked at her with warmth and kindness. She felt as if she had known him and loved him all her life. When he was gone, she sat slumped down in her seat, hardly aware of what was going on in the circus ring, or of Uncle George's muttered protests at having been made a spectacle of. She knew that something important had just happened to her.

2

Uncle George decided that he would try to get some backstage pictures of this circus after all. Aunt May had suggested that he could do something with the idea of provincial troupes. Liza went with them in the hope of seeing the clown. She knew that she had to see him again.

When they found the dressing-room area, a man stopped them and asked in Russian what they wanted. Uncle George summoned his best smile and tried to explain in English that he wanted to take some pictures. He showed the man his camera. The man shook his head, frowning.

"*Niet, niet.*" He took Uncle George's arm, although Uncle George was still talking.

Liza was scanning the backstage crowd of people,

looking for the clown. She was hardly aware of Uncle George's difficulties until Aunt May seized her arm.

"Help him, Liza! Explain to the man!"

Liza saw the clown. He was standing in the hallway talking to another man. Girls in tights, men in their colorful costumes swarmed around and past him.

"Liza!"

"Oh!" She saw that Uncle George was being propelled toward the entrance. She stepped up to the doorman and explained as well as she could in Russian that her uncle wanted to take some pictures for an American book.

The man let go of Uncle George's arm, but barred his way. Politely he explained to Liza that it was not allowed to take pictures unless there was permission from the Ministry of Culture.

Liza translated for Uncle George.

"Tell him your father was a U.S. consul . . ." Uncle George began.

Liza thanked the doorman and looked back over her shoulder. The clown was no longer in sight. She followed Uncle George and Aunt May out into the street. "It's not allowed," she told them.

"You didn't tell them about your father."

"Of course not. What has that to do with it?"

Uncle George was angry. "You could help if you wanted to."

"I did help. I told him what you wanted." She didn't like being spoken to like that. It was vulgar to stand on the sidewalk and argue. She turned away.

Uncle George grabbed her arm. "Don't you ignore me when I'm talking to you!"

A couple going by turned to look at him and then at

Liza. She felt humiliated. In a cool, even voice, she said, "You may as well understand this. I would help you if I could do it myself, but I will never make use of my father's name to help you." She took his hand from her arm, and before he could answer, slipped away in a crowd of people who came along the sidewalk from the circus. She heard Aunt May call her, but she didn't answer. They could get back to the hotel by themselves. At least Uncle George could say the name of the hotel to the taxi driver. He wasn't all that helpless.

She stayed in the crowd as it moved along the boulevard, most of them heading for the entrance to the underground. She didn't have a plan except that for the moment she wanted to escape Uncle George and Aunt May. She went down into the underground, stopped to look at the covers of the magazines displayed in the closed kiosk, and came up to the surface again.

Hardly anyone paid any attention to her, and those who did only gave her a friendly smile. She was tall for her age and used to independence. People usually took her for an adult, although she was not quite seventeen.

She went down a side street, to make sure she didn't run into Uncle George and Aunt May. It was a wide street, with no one on the sidewalks, getting dark now, in that peculiar twilight of early summer in the North. She thought of the dark street in Washington where her father had been shot. But street crime in the Soviet Union was almost nonexistent. She had seen the patrols of volunteer citizens who helped to keep it that way.

Almost without being aware of it, she was walking back toward the circus. When she got to the backstage entrance, almost everyone seemed to have gone. She sat down on a bench a little way off and waited.

After ten or fifteen minutes, the clown came out. She recognized him at once although he was in street clothes. The man she had seen him talking to was with him, and they were still deep in conversation. The clown turned once and looked behind him as if he thought someone might be there, but there was no one. He glanced toward Liza when they passed the bench, but she was sitting in shadow and he gave no sign of recognition.

For a few seconds she watched them going up the street. Then she got up and followed them. On the main boulevard there were still quite a few people. She kept the clown and his friend in sight without getting too close to them. Once she almost lost them when she got caught up in a group of people pushing their way toward a bus stop. She was always surprised at the sheer bulk of many Muscovites, both men and women. They moved along like bulldozers, and it was almost impossible to make any headway against them. She found herself caught between two broad, muscular women and a man, who were talking and laughing and apparently quite unaware that they were moving her along with them. When she wriggled free of them, for a moment she could not see the clown.

She felt panicky. She didn't know why she was following him, but she couldn't stop. He pulled her along like a magnet. She saw him just as he turned a corner and hurried after him.

They were walking quickly, and there were no crowds on this side street. She lingered in the shadows of the buildings until they were almost a block ahead of her. In a few minutes they turned into a lighted café. She slowed down even more until she reached the place.

Through the window she could see them. They were at a corner table. Half a dozen other people were in there, having tea and something to eat. The clown was facing the counter with its big samovar, and his friend faced the window where Liza stood. They were not near any of the other customers, but both of them glanced at the others from time to time.

The clown seemed worried or anxious. It distressed Liza. When he had looked at her in the circus, his eyes had seemed so clear and free of trouble. And in the ring, of course, he had seemed carefree and almost bubbling with humor and joy. She couldn't bear it to see him worried. She longed to know what was troubling him.

They were drinking glasses of tea and eating piroshki. The man with the clown got up and got them more hot piroshki. The clown ate as if he were hungry. Liza wondered if he had had any dinner. He is so thin, she thought; he should eat more.

It began to rain again, and she turned up her collar. She had not worn a hat. She studied the profile of the clown, trying to read all she could in it. When she moved forward a little to see him better, as the rain streaked the glass, the other man looked directly at her. She was sure he had seen her.

A police car came along the street and slowed near her. She started to walk along the sidewalk, but it came alongside her and the officer called to her in Russian. She went up to him and answered him in English.

"I have been to the circus. I'm looking for the taxi stand."

"Taxi?" He laughed and pointed back up the street.

"Boot'," he said. And when she didn't understand, he repeated, "Boot'." He pointed to her rain-drenched head.

She still wasn't sure what he meant, but she thanked him and started back up the street in the direction he had pointed. As she passed the café, the clown's friend was standing in the doorway looking out. She hurried on her way.

At the head of the street, where it joined the boulevard, she saw the shelter next to the taxi stand, and she realized that the policeman had been speaking in English. "Booth," he had said. She waved a taxi down in a couple of minutes and went back to the hotel.

It was almost midnight when she let herself into her room. She tried to be quiet but Aunt May, in her housecoat, knocked on the door almost at once.

"Where on earth have you been?" She was plainly annoyed. "I was worried to death."

"That's silly," Liza said. "You don't need to worry about me."

"Liza." Aunt May's usually soft mouth was tight. "I know you know your way around, probably better than we do, but you are still a minor and I am responsible for you. During the day, all right, but I will not have you roaming the streets in the middle of the night. Do you understand?"

"All right, Aunt May." She just wanted her to go away.

"You were rude to your uncle."

"If I was rude, I'm sorry." It was the best thing to say, to avoid a lot of arguing.

Aunt May looked as if she didn't believe it. "He's trying hard to get this book together. It means a lot to him."

"I know."

"Well, try to be a little sympathetic."

"All right, Aunt May."

Aunt May gave her a long, irritated stare, and then said abruptly, "Good night."

Liza locked the door, got into her pajamas, and knelt by the window, looking out at the rain-blurred lights of the city. She wished she knew what the Clown was worried about. It wasn't right for a clown to have to worry. Especially her Clown.

3

Liza woke early and lay staring up at the ceiling, thinking about the Clown. Now in daylight it seemed crazy that she had trailed a young man she didn't even know and had even spied on him. It wasn't the kind of thing she did, giving way to impulses like that. The best thing she could do, she told herself, was to forget the whole business.

She listened to the crashing and squawking of the noisy plumbing and finally got up and took a shower. When she was dressed, she went to the buffet on the same floor. It wasn't open, so she walked down two flights until she found one that was. She got a glass of tea and a caviar sandwich. She liked having a caviar sandwich for breakfast because it was something she would never do anywhere else.

Maybe, she thought, that was why she had followed the Clown. Like eating caviar for breakfast, it was something she wouldn't do anywhere else. Maybe it was the effect Moscow had on her. The Russians seemed so interesting and bizarre, their city, themselves, the things that went on, the extreme contrasts between an old man in Mongolian peasant clothes and a spruce young Red Army soldier, or between the little centuries-old chapels and the huge modern slab of hotel she was in, which housed six thousand guests. Nothing was the way you expected it to be. Perhaps including herself.

To get her mind off the Clown, she thought about what she would do during the day. Perhaps go to see the Historical Museum, which they had missed last time. Or an art gallery. The main thing was to stay out of Uncle George's way. They wouldn't be up yet, and they always ate in the dining room rather than the buffet because Uncle George thought he didn't get his money's worth for his meal vouchers in the buffet. He'd rather face the long delays and the bad service downstairs. Uncle George worried a lot about getting his money's worth.

She smiled, remembering his annoyance at her having "all that money." She would have to remember to tell that to Harriet and Walter. They would be amused. Her father had left the house in Virginia to them, with enough money to run it. The rest of the money was in trust for Liza, but it was no fortune. If Uncle George weren't so dense, he'd know that old plantation families had lost most of their money a long, long time ago: although her father said they never quite believed it themselves.

She had spent little time in America, but she remembered one cold Christmas when they had all huddled around the fireplace in her grandparents' big, drafty parlor, and she had asked her father to give them her allowance for a Christmas present so they could buy wood or coal for the fireplaces in all the other rooms. There was no central heating. Her father had not laughed. He explained that keeping the whole house operating in winter not only took lots of expensive fuel but servants to take care of things, and all they had was old Peter, who was too bent and stiff for any hard work. Her memory of her grandparents had remained from that Christmas: two gentle, nice people sitting near the fire with a screen behind them, Grandmother forever working on a crocheted bedspread in spite of arthritic fingers, and Grandfather studying the financial pages, especially cotton prices, although they hadn't grown cotton on the place since he was a boy.

She wished she had had a chance to be with them more. Her father had planned to send her to Virginia for the summer when she was nine, but then her mother got sick and he thought she shouldn't go. The following year, when her mother insisted she should, the grandparents died suddenly within a few weeks of each other, before it was time for her to leave. She had not been there since.

Her father would have liked the Clown. He had always valued kindness, and that was what she had seen in the Clown's eyes. People, her father had always said, didn't care enough about each other.

She finished her tea and left the buffet. If she went back to her room, she might run into Aunt May. She decided to go on downstairs and out for a walk. She rang for the lift.

It was a warm, sunny day, a Saturday, and the streets were thronged. She walked across the open expanse of Red Square and was scolded by the traffic policeman because she forgot to stop at the avenue used by official cars. No cars were in sight, and no private cars were allowed, but if you were supposed to stop, you should stop. She said she was sorry, and he waved her on.

The usual endless line stretched away from Lenin's tomb, far back out of sight in the grounds of the Kremlin. It moved very slowly. She wondered why they did it. It seemed like a kind of religious observance, although the Russians wouldn't like that interpretation of it. When she crossed back from the Kremlin toward the GUM department store, she saw an old man in a dusty smock, a turban, and cloth puttees, carrying a little bundle of something over his shoulder and smoking a cigarette. He stopped to look at the line of people shuffling toward the tomb. A policeman spoke to him, and the old fellow stared at him with pale blue eyes.

Curious, Liza edged closer. The policeman was explaining, politely, that one was not allowed to loiter there. The old man just looked at him, not at all intimidated, saying nothing. Liza wondered if he even knew Russian. She remembered her father saying that some of the older people in the far-off republics had never bothered to learn it. The policeman motioned to the man's cigarette. No smoking here. The man took the cigarette out of his mouth, looked at it, put it back in his mouth, turned his back on the policeman and put one foot on the stanchion that separated Red Square from the street.

Liza pretended not to be watching, but she kept them in sight. She was afraid the policeman would arrest the old man, who looked dusty and tired, as if he had come a long way. Dusty and tired but not at all daunted by official Moscow. The policeman looked at him for a moment, then laughed, shrugged, and walked away.

She thought of buying something for Harriet and Walter in GUM, but inside her one thought was to get out. The wide arcade that ran the length of the store was so solidly packed with people she could hardly move. Once she got swept into the food department quite without wanting to go there, and it took her several minutes to fight her way out. The crowd was good-natured, happy with the beautiful weather, but it frightened her a little to get trapped that way.

When she finally got outside again, she was breathless and her hair was flying in all directions. She took the subway passage under the street intersection and walked along the sidewalk that bordered the far side of the Kremlin. There were fewer people here. A woman tried to sell her something that looked like lottery tickets, and a man with a little pushcart, who sold fruit drinks, gave her a hopeful smile, but she shook her head.

She began to think of the Clown again, trying to imagine what pressures and problems a circus performer might have. Or perhaps it was more personal. Maybe his wife didn't love him anymore or his girl wouldn't marry him or someone he loved had died. Yet his expression had been worry more than grief, when she watched him backstage and at the café. As if whatever it was was happening now, or going to happen. She wished she could help him. He had made her happy; she would like to make him happy.

Without consciously heading that way, she found herself after a while in the vicinity of the circus building. She went up the steps and looked at the posters. She studied for a long time the picture of the two clowns. It was a close-up, and the tall Clown's eyes had the same warm, almost affectionate look that she had seen in the auditorium when he looked at her.

It was Saturday. There was a matinee. She went up to the box office window and bought a ticket. Then she found the café and went in. The girl behind the counter looked surprised when Liza ordered. It was not a place where tourists came. The girl took particular care to find Liza a good, hot piroshki, and she smiled at her and said something Liza didn't understand. There was the inevitable exchange of "thank you" and that word the Russians use for "you're welcome" or "excuse me" or, it seems, any other gap in the conversation. Liza sat down and ate slowly, watching the door.

There was no reason to believe that the Clown always ate there, but she kept her eyes open, just in case. She wondered if he would be annoyed if he noticed that she hung around. It couldn't go on very long anyway because she would be here only a few more days. She felt strangely lonely at the idea of leaving without knowing the Clown at all, probably without speaking to him. She didn't understand why she should feel that way, but she did. She would never be able to explain it to anyone, not even to Mademoiselle, because she couldn't explain it to herself.

She had a second glass of tea and lingered over it as long as she could. There was no sign of the Clown. She got up at last, smiled at the girl behind the counter, thanked her and left. There were still several hours before the circus would begin. She decided to go back to the hotel and change into the dress she'd bought just before she left Zurich at the end of the school term. She had never worn it. After the performance maybe she'd get up nerve enough to go back to the stage door and ask the Clown to autograph her program. Lots of people did that. He wouldn't think that was strange. He might even talk to her for a minute. She could tell him how much she enjoyed his performance. Once when she lived in London her mother had taken her backstage to meet Miss Angela Lansbury. People did it all the time.

Pleased with her idea, she found a taxi and went back to the hotel. Just hanging around waiting for a glimpse of the Clown made her nervous. It would be much better to do something.

As soon as she opened her door, her aunt came out of her own room and called to her. She was agitated.

"Liza, where have you been? I've been frantic. I must talk to you."

Liza's stomach muscles tightened. She had had too many disasters in her life not to feel frightened by the threat of any crisis. "What's the matter?"

"I've got to go home at once. My father has died."

Liza sat down on her bed. "We're going right away?"

Aunt May gave her an odd look. "I know you didn't know him, but you could say you're sorry or something."

"I *am* sorry. Really I am." It had been brutal of her, but her only reaction had been that she wouldn't see the Clown again.

Aunt May seemed satisfied with that. "I had a cable

early this morning. I couldn't find you anywhere. You must go out at dawn." She looked in the mirror absently and fussed with her hair. "I've had a terrible morning."

"I'm sorry," Liza said dutifully, again, but she had never had the impression that Aunt May felt close to her father.

"Well, not just the grief, of course, but trying to get out of this incredible country. You wouldn't believe . . ." She glanced toward the set of electrical outlets and checked herself. "Of course it's their busy season, and they had trouble finding me a plane reservation. They said at first they couldn't do it, but I wept and carried on . . ." She paused again. "I mean, I am grief-stricken. My own father." She dabbed at her eyes with a Kleenex.

"I've heard it's very hard to change your itinerary." Aunt May did look pale and Liza felt remorseful. She shouldn't assume that Aunt May wasn't grief-stricken about her father. What if someone had thought that about her? "Is there anything I can do?"

Aunt May looked pleased. "Yes, dear, there really is. You see, I tried and tried to get your flight changed, too. I knew you wouldn't want to stay here without me." As she said it, the unlikelihood of its being true seemed to strike her. "Well, I mean it doesn't seem suitable. George has to stay to finish his work, you see, and he'll be very busy . . ."

And he doesn't want me on his hands, Liza thought.

"But those . . . I couldn't get Intourist to change your ticket. Liza . . ." She lowered her voice. "They get you in this room with nothing in it but a desk and a straight chair, and you stand in front of the desk like an unruly schoolchild . . . There's this overhead light with a single bulb . . . It's like . . ." She picked up the pen on Liza's desk and wrote on the back of an envelope: "Like a concentration camp or something." She showed the envelope to Liza and then tore it in little pieces. "Anyway, enough of that. I am flying out at 2:30. Now, about George. You know how impractical he is."

Liza nodded. Uncle George was the only person she'd ever known who could mislay both his ticket and his passport just as he was coming through customs.

"I hope you'll keep an eye on him. Don't let him know it, you know."

"What do you want me to do?" She had no wish to baby-sit Uncle George.

Aunt May became businesslike. "I've made a list of the things he is to do, and you'll have to remind him each day. Best make a new list for each of the remaining days. Otherwise he'll get all mixed up, he always does." She consulted a neatly printed list. "Today he's having lunch with a young chap he met in the bar, a film actor. He thinks he can get George permission to take some pictures on the set. I don't know when that will be but check with George and write it down. Now, allowing for that, his other activities . . . let's see. Tomorrow he goes on the Intourist tour to Kolomenskoye. I don't know if he can find anything there in the way of old theaters or not but it's worth a try. That's in the afternoon. Leave downstairs at one o'clock."

"Aunt May, do you mean I should trail around after him every minute and see he gets where he's supposed to be?"

"No, no, of course not. George isn't a complete idiot after all. He tries hard. He's just disorganized. If you slip his day's itinerary under his door in the morning, he'll follow it. Now Monday . . . yes, Monday I thought he could go to the Palace of Culture. I spoke to Intourist, and the girl will arrange it for the morning."

"Which Palace of Culture? There's one for every big factory and every profession."

Aunt May interrupted impatiently. "I know, dear. Intourist will tell him. They always have a theater, you know. If he can't do the big well-known theaters, then he'll have to slant another way and do the less-known ones. Now that leaves Tuesday, because you leave Tuesday night. Tuesday I think he should go out to the All-Union Agricultural and Industrial Exhibition. They have a theater there. He could go by trolleybus, but knowing George, he'd better take a cab. Well, that does it. Remind him to pack Tuesday morning. You pick up the plane tickets from Intourist Monday morning." She pulled a folder out of her bag. "I'll leave his passport with you. He misplaces it. Now, Liza, he'll spend the night with you in Copenhagen, just as we intended to, and be sure he gets to the Copenhagen airport at 10:00 the next morning. Do those people of yours have a car?"

Liza frowned. Aunt May always spoke of "those people" as if they were serfs or something. "Of course," she said shortly.

"All right, the man can drive George to the airport."

"I'll ask Walter," she said coldly. "If he's not busy."

Aunt May looked irritated. "Well, they do work for you, don't they?"

Liza's newfound sympathy for Aunt May dissolved.

She turned away. "You can leave the list there. Although I would think a grown man could take care of himself."

"He's an artist. Artists are impractical."

"Oh."

"It won't kill you, Liza," Aunt May said sharply. "I can't say that you've put yourself out much for us so far. We did, after all, bring you on this trip."

Liza bit her lip. No sense fighting with Aunt May. It would soon be over, and she could forget about her for another ten years or so.

Aunt May changed her tone again. "We're glad you came, Liza. I hope you've enjoyed it."

"Yes," Liza said. "Thank you for bringing me." It was the best she could do.

Aunt May put her list and the passport on the desk. "We've seen so little of you over the years. You hardly seem like an American girl."

"I suppose."

"Even your accent is English."

"Well, I grew up in England."

Aunt May hesitated. "What about next year? Wouldn't you like to come to the States to school? You could stay with us, you know."

"Oh, no," Liza said quickly. "Thank you very much. I'll be going back to Zurich."

"And those people. Will they stay at the apartment in Copenhagen?"

"Yes."

"Do they like it there? It must seem strange to them. I mean the language and the people and all. Simple country people like them."

35

Liza looked at her to see what she was up to but she couldn't tell. "They love Copenhagen. And they speak as much Danish as I do—which isn't much, but the Danes usually know some English."

"I see. They've come a long way from Virginia, I should say."

Liza didn't trust herself to answer.

"A man shouldn't marry if he's going to wander all over the globe. I told your mother that before she married Philip."

"My mother loved her life," Liza said. She was afraid she was going to lose her temper.

"Oh, my dear." Aunt May smiled and shook her head. "You would be the last to know. London wasn't so bad, but then that last year in Italy, my poor sister, dying in that filthy country so far from home. It made me sick."

"But not sick enough to come see her," Liza said, trying to keep her voice steady.

Aunt May flushed. "Not all of us have the money to jet all over the world when the whim strikes us."

"My mother loved Italy. We all did. When we found the villa outside Florence . . ." She broke off. What was the use. You could never make Aunt May understand anything.

"It seems such a pity now for you to be wasting your money on the apartment in Copenhagen when you're away at school most of the time. It just makes a sinecure for those people. You could just as well stay with us and save all that." She gathered up her purse. "I'm going to write to Mr. Simms about it. He's a practical man; he'll see the reason of it."

Liza felt a pang of alarm. Would Mr. Simms "see it?" He was a banker, after all, her father's friend, her guardian. She would never, never go to live with Aunt May. She had better write Mr. Simms herself, first.

At the door Aunt May turned. She was all smiles now. "Thank you, dear, for looking after your Uncle George. Have a nice time the rest of your stay. Remember, you can pick up the plane tickets from Intourist on Monday. They'll tell you what time to leave."

Liza nodded. There was nothing to say. You couldn't say "have a good trip" under the circumstances. Her aunt went out and shut the door. Liza picked up the list for Uncle George, looked at it, and put it down again. For the first time she felt that they were not just tiresome relatives. They were enemies.

4

Before she changed her clothes Liza wrote to her guardian. She always wrote him every month or so anyway, to let him know how she was getting along. He was an Englishman, a banker at Barclay's, who had been at the University of Virginia graduate school when her father was there. He was a nice man, although rather remote. In her letter she told him about Moscow and about Aunt May's having to leave. "She thinks I should go to school in America and live with her," she wrote, "but I hope I'll never have to do that. Dad wanted me to finish in Zurich and then go to Virginia, and that's what I want to do." She chewed the end of the pen, wondering whether she ought to say any more. Better not, she decided. Don't overreact.

She addressed and stamped the envelope and changed her clothes. She dressed with extra care, although she knew she was being absurd. If the Clown even saw her, he certainly wouldn't notice what she wore. But it pleased her to look her best. She liked clothes, and she welcomed an excuse for dressing up.

When she was ready, she stood back and looked at herself in the long mirror. Her new dress was a lime-green linen, and she was wearing an amber necklace that her father had bought her last year at the shop in the hotel. After she had brushed her hair till it shone, she surveyed herself critically, and then she remembered the TV monitor. She swung around to face the corner of the room where all the mysterious electric outlets were.

"Well, how do I look?" she said aloud. She gathered up her purse and a white sweater, remembered her key, and left the room quickly, before Aunt May could think of something else to pop in for.

Irina was at the floor desk, chatting with the clerk. They both stopped their conversation to tell Liza how pretty she looked. Irina asked her where she was going, but Liza pretended not to understand. The clerk said something about a young man. Liza looked demure, letting them think she had a date with some boy. There was a lot of nodding and "ah-ing" and significant looks before they let her get away. If they ever knew, she thought, when she was safely in the lift, that I've fallen in love with a circus clown. Fallen in love . . . She thought about it. She didn't know whether that was what it was or not. It wasn't anything like the feeling she had had for boys she'd been interested in. It wasn't something she could analyze, or wanted to. It just *was,* and it was beautiful and moving, and that was enough. If she tried to take it apart to see what it consisted of, it might vanish.

She arrived early at the circus and had to wait ten or fifteen minutes before the doors opened. She strolled around to the stage door, just in case, but of course the performers would already be in their dressing rooms getting made up. He would be leaning toward the mirror, carefully applying the spots of rouge to his cheeks, flattening down his hair. She checked her purse to make sure she'd brought a pen for him to sign the program with.

A group of Young Pioneers were lined up at the entrance when she came back. They were chattering and milling around, and when the door opened, they plunged through ahead of her. It might be rather fun to be a Young Pioneer. They had wonderful facilities for anything they were interested in, their own theaters, sports of all kinds, all sorts of things.

She had a good seat in the second row on the aisle. Studying the program, she found she could read some but not all of it. She had taught herself Russian last year from a set of records and had a fair vocabulary in everyday speech, the kind of words tourists needed, but only the haziest idea of the complicated grammar. Someday she would like to study it seriously. She liked languages. She was fluent in French and Italian, but not as good in German.

She watched the audience arriving. Lots of children today. Russians had a talent for enjoying. Last year when she had seen the Bolshoi do *Il Trovatore,* every seat in the big, beautiful opera house had been filled, and the audience was one of the most interested she had ever seen. Today, too, they were waiting excitedly for the performance to start.

She tried to keep her mind on the early acts, but she kept looking toward the entrance on the other side, where the clowns entered. It seemed forever before they came. When she finally saw that tall, skinny figure in its absurd clothes, she laughed out loud with relief. She had almost been afraid he wouldn't be there. The woman sitting next to her smiled and said something in Russian. Liza was too excited to understand, but she returned the smile.

He seemed as carefree and as gay as he had during yesterday's performance. If he had been worrying later, perhaps the cause had disappeared. She felt relieved. She leaned forward in her seat, watching every move he made. The routine was the same, but it seemed to her there were small differences, little improvisations. During the sketching scene, the first time he galloped across the arena and up into the stands to present the sketch to its subject, he pretended to trip on the steps. His long legs seemed to churn in the air before he caught his balance. The audience roared with laughter.

The show was over so soon she could hardly believe it. She stayed in her seat until most of the crowd had gone, nervous about asking him for his autograph. She had practiced saying it in Russian, but perhaps she ought to say it in English, or maybe both ways. Then if he didn't understand English, he wouldn't be embarrassed. She hoped her Russian was more or less right so he'd know what she was saying. She would say it quickly, first in Russian, then in English, and would hold out the program and the pen at the same time. Surely he would understand what she wanted. What if he said no? What if he was annoyed? Sometimes celebrities hated to be bothered by the public. But she had to chance it. It was the only way she could speak to him.

She went out with the last of the audience and walked slowly around the big building to the stage entrance. People were going in and out. In sudden panic she thought he might already have gone. But that didn't seem likely, unless he was terribly quick at changing his clothes. She sat down on the bench where she had sat the night before.

After some time people began to come out. She recognized the girl who had the horses, and a few minutes later an Oriental-looking girl who was part of the high-wire act. She tensed. Surely he would be along in a few minutes. She folded her hands together to keep from fidgeting.

The man who had been with the Clown yesterday suddenly appeared from the street. He had his hat pulled down and he was walking fast, almost running. He pushed past the doorman and disappeared. Perhaps the Clown was waiting for him. She had hoped he would be alone; it would be easier to speak to him. But that was too much to hope for.

Time passed. Other people came out and went off toward the street, sometimes in groups, chattering and laughing, sometimes in twos or alone. But the Clown didn't come. She began to worry. Could she have missed him? He might have changed his clothes very fast and gotten away before she left the auditorium. She was vexed with herself for having dawdled. Still, it was hard to believe he could have gone so quickly.

She noticed a man sitting on another bench a little further along the walk. He seemed to be waiting, too, although he looked casual enough. As she watched him, he got up and bent down to smell a rose in the plot of bushes next to his bench. When he looked up and saw her watching him, he returned the look for a moment and then sat down again, busying himself with a little notebook that he got from his pocket, making notes of some kind. He looked ordinary enough, in slightly baggy pants and a faded blue cloth jacket. Nothing remarkable about him, and yet he made her a little uneasy.

The Clown's friend came out, alone. When he was near the other bench, the man in the blue jacket got up and spoke to him. The Clown's friend shook his head rapidly, said something, gestured with his hands. Then he walked quickly away. The man in the jacket stood watching him go.

Liza knew she ought to get up and leave, but still she sat there, waiting. She was sure now that the Clown had already gone, either before she got there or out by some other exit. She went up to the door and waited until she caught the old doorman's eye. He smiled and came over to her, saying "good afternoon" in Russian. She asked him if the Clown had left. The tall one. She measured with her hand. The man's expression changed. He was still polite, but the warmth went out of his eyes. He shook his head almost curtly and turned away.

Puzzled, and sorry she had asked, Liza began to walk slowly toward the street. She was so deep in thought, she had forgotten the man on the bench, until he appeared beside her. In Russian he said, "Excuse me, do you have a match?" He had an unlighted cigarette in his hand.

She looked at him. She could still see nothing unusual about him. He had an ordinary face, brown eyes, thin mouth, bad teeth. He was about five feet ten, with muscular shoulders. Probably someone who worked with his hands. He was smiling slightly, a little apologetic about asking for a light. She was quite sure he was not trying to pick her up. And yet he looked at her with more than casual interest.

She shook her head and said in English, "I'm sorry. I don't smoke. I don't have any matches."

He seemed to lose interest in her at once, so perhaps after all he had only wanted a match. He apologized in Russian and turned away. She went on to the boulevard.

She stood on the curb, thinking. Something was wrong, but she didn't know what made her think so or what it could possibly be. Looking back, she saw the man in the jacket walking in the opposite direction, no different from the other people who strolled along the boulevard late on a Saturday afternoon. She must be imagining things. But still she lingered on the sidewalk. Out on the wide boulevard taxis whizzed by at their usual fast speed, making their usual racket. Russians took terrible care of their cars. She wondered if they took care of their planes and tanks and missiles in the same careless way. She saw an empty taxi coming toward her, but she turned away and went back to the circus to buy a ticket for the evening performance. She put it in her purse and left the building, thinking, "I have lost my mind."

She was hardly aware of the early acts at the evening performance. Stiff with anxiety she waited to see if the Clown would appear. When he ran into the ring doffing his ridiculous top hat and beaming at the audience, she felt faint with relief. Everything seemed to be perfectly normal. She sat back and began to enjoy the circus once more. She almost knew the acts by heart now.

At the intermission she joined the surge of people toward the refreshment room. She had been so worried, instead of eating, she'd spent the time between performances walking around and finally sitting in a park watching children play without really seeing them. Performances began at seven, so most people had not had dinner. They ate heartily at intermission, crowding into the big room, calling to the busy waitresses behind the counters, waving their rubles or their handful of kopeks, smiling and talking to each other.

Liza stood in line and filled up her plate with sandwiches, cheese, and sliced cucumbers. As a rule she didn't think much of Russian food, but now she was hungry enough to find it wonderful. She felt excited and happy because her Clown was all right. In her mind she sang the little phrase that her Yorkshire friend Benita was always saying: "Not to worry, not to worry." Perhaps it was because terrible things had happened to the people she loved in the past that she was so quick to expect the worst. She smiled at a couple who had been jostled up against her in the crowd. "Sorry," she said in Russian, "sorry." They laughed, and she laughed. It was a lovely evening.

Before the last of the performers had joined the closing parade around the ring, Liza slipped out. She wasn't going to miss him this time. There was no one outside the stage entrance. She walked around to the other side, looking for another door. There was a small fire exit on the far side. He might have come out that way. But why? Probably just because it was convenient, she told herself. Don't look for trouble.

She came back to the main entrance, deciding she would just have to take a chance that he wouldn't do it again. There was no way she could keep both exits in sight at the same time. She sat this time on the bench farther away, the one where the man in the jacket had sat. Maybe it would bring her luck to change her position.

He was one of the first to come out, and he came alone, walking quickly. Without giving herself time to lose her nerve, Liza jumped up and approached him. He stopped suddenly and took a step backward, as if she had frightened him. He gave no sign of recognition, but she hadn't really expected it.

She held out the program and her pen and said, first in English, then in Russian: "Please, will you sign my program?"

He smiled and took the program and the pen, quickly signing his name. When he gave them back to her, he said, "Thank you, Mademoiselle," in English, and walked away.

She watched him go. A group of young boys called to him. He waved to them but didn't stop. Wherever he was going, he was in a hurry. There had been no chance to talk to him, even to say, "I liked your performance." She was going to have to give up. One couldn't pursue a man for no reason except that one loved his smile. She would go home and let him be.

But she walked out to the street for a last look. A group of people stopped him for a moment, people who had been at the circus. He smiled and nodded and said something, but again he hurried away as soon as he could. She stood under a tree watching him as he turned down the boulevard in the direction of the street where the café was. As she was about to move on, she stopped. A man had stepped out of the shadows and was following the Clown. Although he wore a tan mac instead of the blue jacket, she was sure it was the man who had waited that afternoon. Liza started after him.

There were a lot of people on the boulevard. A large group waited at a bus stop, another crowd headed for the entrance to the underground, some stepped off the curb to wave frantically at the cruising taxis that swerved toward them. Many other people were just out strolling along the street on this warm early summer Saturday night.

Liza lost sight of the Clown, and she saw that the man ahead of her had lost him, too. He stopped uncertainly at the intersection of another street and looked down it, but that street also was well occupied tonight. It was not the street with the café—that was the next one—but there was a milk bar near the corner, where a number of people were heading. The man hesitated, stepped off the sidewalk so he could get a clearer view of the boulevard ahead of him, then jumped hastily back again as a taxi plunged past him to pick up two Red Army officers who had been waving their arms.

Liza stood up against a darkened storefront, out of the mainstream of the crowd, watching the man. She couldn't see the Clown anywhere. He might have jumped into a taxi, or he might have gotten on a bus, or he could have run down into the underground. Or he could have gone back to the café.

The man in the mackintosh hurried on down the boulevard. At the street where the café was, he paused and looked, and then went on again, almost running down the broad sidewalk, keeping close to the curb to get past the sauntering crowds. Liza waited a minute and then she turned down the street toward the café.

Almost every table was full. Liza couldn't see the Clown, but from the sidewalk it was not possible to see all the tables. Some people were standing at the counter, some walking back toward their seats. She went inside and lined up at the counter for a glass of tea.

She didn't turn around until she had her tea. The place was small and tables were close together. After a moment a man at a table in a corner got up and left. It was a table for two. Liza sat down with her back to the wall. Now she could see the other people without seeming to be looking for someone.

At first she didn't see him. Then, leaning forward to take off her sweater, she saw him at a table like her own in the corner near the door.

He leaned his head back against the wall as if he were trying to avoid being visible to passersby, but he kept glancing toward the door. He had a bowl of salad and a glass of tea, but he was not paying much attention to them. From time to time he took a bite of the salad and a sip of tea, but he obviously had something else on his mind. He didn't glance toward Liza's table. The other people in the restaurant didn't seem to know him.

From where she sat, Liza had a better view of the sidewalk than he did. She saw his friend before he saw him. The man paused and glanced in the window before he came in. Then he looked back over his shoulder before he took off his cap, hung it on a nail, and sat down. The Clown looked relieved. They talked for a few minutes in low voices, urgently. Then the man went up to the counter and got some tea. While he waited, he turned and looked around at the other people. When he noticed Liza, he looked startled. She didn't know how to act, so she smiled slightly and nodded. He turned away without responding.

When he was back at his table, he leaned toward the Clown and said something. The Clown turned his head and saw her. He nodded and smiled and then said something to his friend. She was sure he was saying "it's just an admirer" or something like that. But who did they think she might have been? Why were they so nervous? She stirred her tea, trying to decide whether she should tell him about the man who was following him or not. Perhaps the man wasn't really following the Clown at all. She could have imagined it. Perhaps the Clown and his friend were not really worried about anything. She might be dreaming the whole thing, just because she was so concerned about the Clown. The way Harriet always thought Liza was coming down with the flu if she so much as sneezed.

While she sat there wondering what to do, the Clown and his friend were carrying on a conversation in low voices, their heads bent toward each other. The noise of conversation and rattling dishes would have made their words inaudible to anyone else, but from time to time the friend glanced at the adjoining tables, where other customers ate and talked. No one seemed to be paying any attention to them.

I could go over to him, Liza thought, and say there was a man who seemed to be looking for him. Maybe it was an old friend. There was no reason to jump to the conclusion that he was an enemy. Except that everyone seemed so frightfully nervous. Perhaps the Clown was always nervous. Artists were supposed to be temperamental. She couldn't make up her mind what to do. If he was really in danger, it would be awful not to have warned him. Of course, he might not believe her or might think she was being a nuisance. She pressed her hands together in her lap, trying to summon the courage to speak to him.

She leaned forward to put on her sweater, and at the same time glanced toward the window where she had stood the evening before, looking in at the Clown. Someone was looking in now. It was the man in the mac. He did not seem to have seen the Clown, but he would in a minute.

She got up and went to the Clown's table, coming around it so that she stood between him and the window. Both men looked up, startled.

"Mademoiselle?" he said.

"A man has been following you," she said. She repeated it in Russian, knowing she was getting the tense wrong but praying he understood. "He is outside. The door near the counter . . . go there. I will get in his way . . ."

Before she finished, the Clown stood up and moved sideways along the wall toward the lavatory door. Liza moved so that she blocked the view of the man outside. The Clown's friend went on eating, his head down. Several people finished their food and headed for the door, unconsciously helping Liza obstruct the view from outside. When the Clown disappeared, Liza took her tea glass to the counter for more. A new group of people, four young people, came in while she waited for her tea, and a middle-aged couple left. When she had her tea and arrived back at her table, the Clown's friend had gone.

In about five minutes the man in the mac came in and looked around. He saw her and looked at her for a moment as if he were trying to place her. She glanced at him and looked away without recognition. He came over to her.

"We meet again, Mademoiselle," he said in heavily accented English.

She looked up at him blankly. "I'm sorry?"

"We met this afternoon, at the circus. I bother you for match."

"Oh, yes." She made herself look at him coolly although her heart was pounding. She wanted him to go away before the Clown came out. The Clown would be careful; of course he would. But he seemed to be so guileless, and now his friend, who looked after him, was gone.

"You have been to circus again?" He smiled at her with his bad teeth.

It was easy to give him a "none-of-your-business" frown. "Oh, no." She busied herself with the sugar for her tea.

"You are English tourist, Mademoiselle?"

She gave him a cold look. "No, indeed. I am employed at the embassy."

It was the right answer. He looked disconcerted and backed away. "I am sorry, Mademoiselle. Good evening."

She nodded.

After one more sweeping glance around the restaurant he left.

6

The crowd in the café was beginning to thin out. Liza sat at her table a little longer to make sure the man didn't come back. She would have to tell the Clown that the man had gone. Otherwise he wouldn't know and would be afraid to chance coming out.

She got up, picked up her purse, and went to the door, which led to the lavatory. She found herself in a narrow, dimly lit hall, with one door leading into the kitchen, and at the end of the hall a door that looked like the place. There didn't seem to be any back exit. Unless the Clown had managed to get out through the window, if there was one in the lavatory, he must be still there. Whatever it was that he was being chased for, it made her angry that he should have to be humiliated in this way.

53

For a moment she longed to go away and forget the whole thing. There was no way of telling what kind of mess she was getting herself into. But then she thought of the Clown's gentle face, his kind eyes, his smile. She had to help him. Bracing herself, she knocked on the door of the w.c.

"Are you there?" she said in a low voice. "It's all right now."

The door opened and the Clown looked out. When he saw her alone in the hall, he came out and closed the door. He looked past her, up the hall. He seemed to be making a great effort to stay calm but he was very pale.

"Thank you, Mademoiselle," he said.

"He came in but he left again. Your friend is gone, too."

"Yes. Of course." He looked as if he couldn't think what to do.

"I am going back to my hotel in a taxi," she said. "Why don't you come with me? I can let you off wherever you say."

He looked at her searchingly. "You are most kind. But just now . . . I have nowhere to go." He laughed, but it was a desperate-sounding little laugh.

"You have nowhere to stay?"

"I can stay with a friend. But after midnight only. Now it is too early. Too . . . complicated." He pronounced the word carefully, syllable by syllable. "You must not bother for me."

"I would like to bother for you." She heard her voice take on what her father used to call "Liza's coping voice." She didn't want to be officious, but this man obviously didn't know where to turn. "We can walk

54

out of here, up the street, and get a taxi. We can go to my hotel and talk a while out on the terrace until it's safe for you to go to your friend."

He looked bemused. "I make danger for you."

"I don't think so." She smiled at him.

He held out his hands to show her that they were shaking. "I am not a brave man." He tried to return her smile. "No brave man at all."

"My father always said brave was apt to mean foolhardy." She gestured toward the door. "We'd better go before that man comes back." She was talking to him in English because she didn't trust her Russian now when it was important he should understand her. She spoke slowly. "Up the street to taxi. I will do the talking. All right?" She didn't want the taxi driver to notice that she was with a Russian. He might wonder.

"So. I am ready." He straightened his shoulders. She noticed that he had a worn old leather bag with him. He must have checked out of the circus company's quarters. Checked out or faded out or whatever.

She led the way up the hall and into the restaurant. Only five or six people were still there, no one she recognized. She walked on through and out the door without paying any attention to anyone, trying to look perfectly normal, a young man and a girl leaving a restaurant.

There was no one in the street that she could see, except a man on the opposite sidewalk who was kissing a girl. She let the Clown catch up with her, and they walked along in silence to the boulevard. The after-theater crowds had thinned out. It took her only a minute to wave down a taxi. When she told him to go to the Rossia Hotel, she caught the Clown's quick look. She knew he must be wondering if he could trust her.

She settled back and pulled her sweater around her. For the benefit of the driver she said, "You had better not try to talk with that sore throat of yours."

He took his cue. He smiled and turned up the collar of his coat. She saw in the rearview mirror that the driver had noticed. Taxi drivers were always curious. She decided to go on talking as if they were . . . what? A young married couple? No, that would be embarrassing. The Clown was too young to be her father. All right then, uncle and niece. An uncle could be any age.

"Uncle Jack, I told you, you should have worn your sweater on the river yesterday. You really should have." She frowned at him severely. He looked baffled, and she wasn't sure he understood but she kept going. "You know what Aunt Sophie always says: there are germs in the night air. Germs!" She shuddered convincingly. "No, don't argue. You're not to talk until tomorrow."

The Clown gave her a sudden impish grin and made a face. She burst out laughing. This was fun, or would be if there were no danger. Uncle Jack. She wished she knew what kind of danger he was in. Perhaps he would tell her, but probably not. He didn't even know who she was. She could be part of whatever enemy he was fleeing, for all he knew. She gave him a quick sideways glance. Whatever he was wanted for, she knew he was innocent. She had never seen such an innocent-looking person in her life.

The taxi hurtled down narrow side streets as if the devil were after it. Moscow streets always seemed eerie, she thought, because there were so few private cars.

All that wide network of new boulevards and old winding streets, and hardly anyone using them except taxis and army vehicles.

The driver turned with a squeal of tires into an alley, which led through a stone archway into a cobblestone courtyard. The clown was looking out the window intently. He seemed worried. But then the taxi shot out again through another narrow arch onto Razin Street and up the steep ramp to the hotel. It braked to a jolting stop at the north entrance.

Liza had the right change and the tip already in her hand. When she and the Clown were on the sidewalk in front of the revolving door to the lobby, the taxi pulled up a little further and parked.

"Why does he wait?" the Clown said nervously.

"To pick up another fare." She took him along the pavement that bordered the enormous hotel. "We'll go around to the river side." They walked in silence past one of the restaurants, past another lobby, around the corner of the foreign currency shop where her father had bought the amber necklace for her such a long time ago. The walk was dimly lighted and there were no other people until they came to the riverfront entrance. Here there were some taxis waiting for fares, and occasionally a taxi arrived to unload guests.

Liza led him away from the lobby entrance toward the river, which flowed wide and dark below them. Near the river, Liza found a bench under a tree. She sat down. "There," she said. She wanted to say "we made it" but she didn't know whether he would understand that expression.

He sat in silence for a few minutes looking out at the

velvet blackness of the river. Occasionally the blackness was lit up by the lights of a passing boat. "It is beautiful city," he said softly.

"Yes. Very beautiful."

"I had forgotten. I was here when I was in circus school, but I have not come since." He sighed.

He was silent for so long, she wondered if she ought to go away. Then he turned and looked back at the huge concrete slab of the hotel. "All tourists . . ." He smiled at her. "All English like you?"

"I'm not English. I'm American."

He was startled. "American? But you speak . . ."

"I grew up in England. I've never really lived in America. But I am American."

He studied her in bewilderment. "You are American, but you don't live in America?"

"No. My father was with the consular service. We have always lived abroad."

"Ah. Your father, whose picture I draw . . ."

She was pleased that he remembered, but she couldn't have him thinking Uncle George was her father. "No, that was my uncle. My father is dead." It was always hard to say it but she had learned to do it.

"Ah. I am sorry."

She looked away. "Thank you." She couldn't endure much sympathy.

He seemed to sense it. Quickly he said, "You know so well what to do. You have experience of many kinds, yes?"

"Well, some kinds."

After a pause he said, "Here we face south, yes?"

"I think so."

"South to Georgia." He took a long breath. "I will not see Georgia again." His voice trembled.

"Why not?"

Again there was a long wait before he answered. "I am to be arrested. That man you save me from, he is KGB."

She gasped. She had heard and read about the KGB, the Russian secret police that blanketed the entire, huge country with its efficient network of spies, a domestic police force with absolute power. "Why you?"

He turned a little so he could look directly at her. "I am a Jew. Georgian Jew. I applied for exit visa. I was a fool. I thought they would give it to me."

"They're after you for that?"

"Yes. My brother . . . my older brother died in mental hospital. Mental?" Not sure of the word, he tapped his head.

"Yes."

"He was put there in mental hospital at Stolboraya, because he spoke up for freedom." He tilted his head up in a momentary flash of pride. "We Georgians, we speak out. It is our way. The Russians do not like us. We give them much trouble."

"My father loved Georgia."

"So?" He looked pleased. "We are different, yes. Very old empire. In Georgia we are still very angry with our king who gave in to Russia. We go back very far, to early Greece, early Rome. It was first Christian empire in the world . . ." He broke off and made a helpless gesture with his left hand. "But why talk of this?"

Liza was moved. Her own sense of a native land was not strong, and for that reason she found other people's

59

love of country very appealing. But if the secret police were after him, this was no time for sentiment. "Are you sure they're going to arrest you?"

"Yes. They have been question my friends. Some have turned away from me in fear, one or two warn me."

"If that man was planning to arrest you, why didn't he do it at the circus?"

He shrugged. "Who knows. They do not like fuss in public place. Some people know me. Clowns, people like clowns sometimes."

Liza tried to think of something. "This friend you're going to stay with tonight, are you safe there?"

He shrugged again. "For two, three night. Too long makes danger for him."

"Has the circus left?"

"Monday. To Leningrad for one week, then home."

"And you won't be with them," she thought. She could feel how much it hurt him.

"Was your exit visa supposed to be for Israel?"

"Yes. It was the only chance."

"Do you want to go to Israel?"

"I just wanted . . . away. I am not Zionist, no."

Somewhere in the back of her mind a scheme was beginning to take shape but it was so wild, she didn't want to think about it directly yet. She looked at her watch. It was ten minutes of twelve.

"Will you promise me something?"

"Anything."

"Will you meet me here tomorrow night at eight o'clock?"

He smiled wryly. "If I'm still free."

"Can you stay in your friend's place during the day?"

He shook his head. "He shares with other people."

She thought. "Why don't you go to the Lenin State Library and stay all day? That's a safe place to be. You know where it is, on Kalinin Street?"

"Yes, I know."

"Have some project so it will look normal. Take a pencil and paper and make notes. Read in some particular field, you know, like English country music or the Spanish Inquisition. But not circuses."

He shook his head admiringly. "You are clever girl."

"No, I've just been on my own a lot. I'm a schemer. Once I cut P.E. for a whole term by pretending to do research on James Boswell. I finally got so fond of Boswell, I did a paper on him." She laughed although she wasn't sure he had followed all that. "You will be here at 8:00? You promise?"

He stood up, smiling. "Promise." He didn't look so frightened now. "I may thank you?"

"No," she said, "I haven't done anything . . . yet."

He stood a moment longer looking at her. Then he walked away along the river road, striding on his long legs. Just before he disappeared from her sight, he looked back, waved, did a quick little dance step like the one he did in the circus. And then he was gone.

Liza went up to her room. She had a lot of thinking to do.

She hadn't thought of Uncle George for hours, but she found a note from him on her bed. He must have gotten her key from the clerk and let himself in. She didn't like the idea. Or perhaps Irina had brought it in for him. She read it.

> Liza,
> Please ask the desk to call me at 8:30. I can't make the idiot at the switchboard understand me. Also did May leave you a list of my activities? Pls. let me have. Also do something about my laundry.
>
> *Unc. Geo.*

Thinking how awful it must be to be married to Uncle George, Liza picked up the phone and left the message for the morning call. Then she consulted Aunt May's list. On a piece of paper she wrote the instructions for going to Kolomenskoye. She added a note that she would get in touch with the laundress. She could imagine how his room must look, without Aunt May there to pick up after him. What a baby he was.

After she got into bed, she lay back on the pillows with her bed lamp still on. She had to work out something. She could not let the Clown be arrested. The idea of his spending his life in a hospital for the mentally ill was unbearable. There must be some way of smuggling him out of the country. She knew people sometimes could get false passports but that was a very tricky business and you would have to know where to go and whom to ask. In Russia, of all places, it would be impossible for anyone who didn't know the ropes.

Nothing practical occurred to her. Tomorrow was Sunday; not much time left. She couldn't ask advice from her father's friends because whatever she did was going to be illegal. She got her address book and looked up Meredith Johnson, a junior secretary at the embassy, who had taken Liza to lunch twice last year, at times when Liza's father was busy. She was very young and nice. Liza could think of no way Meredith could help, but it might not hurt to see her. She usually avoided people who had known her father because it was hard for her to see them, but Meredith was tactful. She would call and ask her to have tea somewhere.

She put out the light, but couldn't get to sleep. She kept seeing the Clown's sad smile, his expression when he spoke of not seeing Georgia again, and the irrepressible merriment that bubbled up even when he was worried. If she could only get him out of the country. He might be unhappy—Russians felt awfully attached to their country—but at least he would be safe. To her the world was home, not any one country. The past was her home, the memory of happy times with her father. The apartment in Copenhagen that her father had found, his room, Harriet and Walter, these were home. She wondered if the Clown had a family besides his brother.

She fell asleep at last, but she awoke early and slipped the note for Uncle George under his door. It was a beautiful summer day. She walked along the river and then went to the National Hotel to have breakfast. It was an old hotel, nicer than the Rossia. Her father had wanted to stay there last year, but it had been full.

A leisurely breakfast made her feel better. There had to be an answer to the Clown's problem. She was not going to let him be destroyed. Occasionally in the London *Times* she had seen pictures of Russians who had been arrested and imprisoned or sent to a psychiatric hospital because they had applied for an exit visa. The Clown was not going to turn into one of those pictures. She had always believed that if you wanted to solve a problem badly enough, you could do it. She opened her purse and looked at Uncle George's passport. Passport pictures always made people look like convicts or something. Uncle George was grinning like an idiot, and his tie was crooked. Place of birth, it said: Detroit, Michigan. Date of birth: April 2, 1936. That would make him, she guessed, perhaps a dozen years older than the Clown. Color of hair: lt. brown. Actually Uncle George's hair was very pale, like straw, but you couldn't tell in the picture, especially since he had so little left in front. The Clown's hair was darker and he didn't have sideburns, but that wouldn't matter. Sideburns could be shaved off. The Clown's eyes were dark brown. On the passport, beside Color of eyes, it said blue.

She studied the passport, trying to think. Height: six feet. The Clown must be six two. Weight: 169 pounds. She couldn't remember how pounds translated into stone, but in any case a man could have lost weight. Uncle George was quite a different shape from the Clown, heavier, thicker in the neck, broader-shouldered. She closed her purse as the waiter came to refill her coffee cup. "What am I thinking of?" she asked herself. How would it be possible to use Uncle George's passport? It wouldn't be, of course. But if only it were . . . She thought they might be able to get away with it. If they could only go right now. But the reservations were for Tuesday, and Intourist made quite sure that you went when you were supposed to. You couldn't just change your mind.

When she got back to the hotel, it was almost noon and Uncle George had gone out. She picked up his key at the desk and went to his room to take care of the laundry. As she had expected, it was a shambles. Uncle George always dropped on the floor whatever he took off. She gathered up his clothes, making a pile of the things that needed washing. She hung up his gray tweed jacket and the dark blue mackintosh that were hanging half on a chair, half on the floor. The maid hadn't been in yet so nothing had been tidied up. What a messy man! She told the desk clerk about the laundry to be picked up and then she went to her own room and washed her hands thoroughly. She felt almost sorry for Aunt May.

It took several calls to get Meredith at her flat but when she did, Meredith sounded pleased. She must come to tea at the flat. Four o'clock. Looking forward to it.

A few minutes before 4:00, Liza told the guard at the gate whom she was visiting and he nodded her into the huge building where foreign press people and minor diplomatic personnel lived. Liza remembered where Meredith's apartment was.

Meredith greeted her warmly. "I was so surprised. I had no idea you were here."

"Only for a few days. I'm with my aunt and uncle. Or at least I was. I am only with my uncle now. My aunt had to go home for a family emergency."

"I hope your uncle is fun."

Liza made a face, and Meredith laughed.

"If I know you, Liza, you'll strike out on your own and have fun anyway. Are you coming over to the embassy?"

Liza looked down. "No, I don't think so."

"Well, they'd be glad to see you, but I know how you must feel. You find a tape you'd like to hear while I rustle us up some tea."

Liza had known Meredith would be nice. Last year they had had one very pleasant hour playing Meredith's Dixieland jazz tapes. While Meredith rattled around in the tiny kitchen now, Liza looked through the tapes and picked out one of Sharkey Bonano's. She loved Dixieland and one of the things she wanted to do when she went to America was to go to New Orleans and spend night after night on Bourbon Street, before the great jazzmen all were gone. Her mother had gone to Sophie Newcomb College and she used to tell Liza wonderful tales of the French Quarter and the old plantations along the river.

When Meredith brought the tea and some little watercress sandwiches that reminded Liza of England, they were quiet for a while, just enjoying the tea and the music. Then they talked about different things, Liza's school year, whether she was still living in Copenhagen. Once or twice Meredith mentioned Liza's father but only in an easy natural way, like: "I remember your father telling us about the people who look after you. They sounded so great." And it was easy then for Liza to talk about Walter and Harriet.

"My uncle is supposed to be doing a book, a picture book, on Russian theater," she said after a while. "He's a photographer. But he's so inept. He never did get his contacts straight so nobody will let him in." She laughed. "He misplaced both his plane ticket and his passport when we came in."

"Oh, dear. Found them again, I hope."

"Oh, yes." Liza paused. "What happens if you lose your passport anyway?"

"Oh, there's a lot of red tape. One contacts the embassy, of course, and we get them a temporary passport. But it's all quite a bore."

"They don't throw you in jail or anything."

"Oh, no. Not if you really had one." She poured some more tea for Liza. "If your uncle wants to try something different, I have a friend who works at the Teatr Mimiki i Zhesta, which is a fascinating place. The actors are deaf-mutes. Boris isn't, though, and he's a doll; I know he'd do what he could for your uncle. He might not be able to take his own pictures, but he could probably get some press pictures. And at least he'd get an interesting story."

"That sounds fine."

"They do dance and pantomime and really they're marvelous." She went to her desk and wrote a name on a slip of paper. "Here, I'd better put down the address, too. I'll call Boris tomorrow and tell him your uncle might show up. All right?"

"Uncle George will be thrilled."

"Good. What's his last name?" She wrote down "George Asher" on another piece of paper, and "CALL BORIS." "I won't forget."

"Thank you so much, Meredith."

"My pleasure. I wish I knew more people. He should have contacted the Ministry of Culture."

"Oh, he did, but they didn't answer him. He's not very well known or anything."

"He could probably take some pictures inside the Kremlin Theater, too, if he asked permission there. In the auditorium, I mean. It's the one near the Spassky Gate. It has earphones to translate into foreign languages."

Liza made a note of it. "I'll tell him."

When Liza was leaving, Meredith said, "Next time let me know ahead. I'd love to take you to the Slavyansky Bazaar for dinner. They have pretty good jazz. But I'm leaving tomorrow afternoon for a twenty-four-hour break at the *dacha*." She stretched and yawned. "And not a minute too soon."

Liza remembered the pleasant *dacha* in the country that the embassy used. She and her father had gone out there for a picnic. And in her mind she made a note: Meredith would be gone until Tuesday night.

About 6:30 Uncle George knocked on her door. She was just back. He looked hot and tired as he came in and sat down on her bed.

"Well, we did that one," he said.

"Was it interesting?" Liza asked politely. She hated having him in her room. But she felt a little sorry for him, he looked so disheveled.

He shrugged. "All right if you go for ancient history. I didn't get much of a story. So they've got this theater." He gestured, palms up. "Big deal." He looked at her. "Listen, this movie character that I met, we didn't get anywhere yet, but he just might be able to get me on the set either in the morning or Tuesday. What am I doing tomorrow?"

Liza looked at Aunt May's list. "Intourist has set up a tour to a Palace of Culture. They have some kind of theater."

"What's for Tuesday?"

"The All-Union Agricultural and Industrial Exhibition."

He made a face. "I could put that one off till Wednesday."

"Wednesday?"

"Yeah. I know that's the day we go, but we don't go till evening, do we?"

Liza hesitated for just a moment. "That's right."

"All right. Then I'll make arrangements to go out to

the movie location with Igor on Tuesday. Write it down. Lord, I can't remember all this stuff."

"I will," she said.

"Now. Tonight I made a date to take Igor to dinner. You know, butter him up. Where shall I take him?"

Liza thought for a minute. "The Praga is nice, and it has a roof garden. It's Czech food."

"I suppose it costs an arm and a leg."

"I think you can use your meal vouchers. Do you want me to make a reservation for you?"

He looked surprised. "That would be fine, Liza. Seven-thirty."

Liza looked up the number and made the reservation.

He got up. "I suppose I won't understand a word on the menu."

"Ask the waiter what he suggests."

He raised his eyebrows. "You're a very hep kid, Liza."

Liza's mind was racing. "Uncle George," she said, as he opened the door to leave. "I was talking to a friend of mine at the embassy. She knows someone at the Teatr Mimiki i Zhesta who might help you get some pictures."

Uncle George brightened. "Now you're talking. What theater?"

"It's a theater where the actors are deaf-mutes."

"Oh, come off it. You're putting me on."

"No, really. It's very popular, very good. You could probably get a marvelous story. I mean it's so different." Slow down, slow down, she thought. Don't overdo it.

"Different is right. This guy your friend knows, do I talk to him in sign language or something?"

"No, he isn't a deaf-mute. I have his name and the address here. I'll get it all down for you. For . . ." She hesitated again. "Tuesday night?"

"Sure, okay. Fine. I'll give it a whirl. Write down all the dope for me." He shook his head. "Deaf-mutes yet." He went out.

Liza sank down in the armchair and leaned her head back. He thought they were leaving on Wednesday. Uncle George the Bumbler. If she didn't say anything, he would be at the Teatr Mimiki when the plane left for Copenhagen. It was a rotten trick to play on him, really rotten, but on the other side of the balance was the Clown's life. She closed her eyes and began to plan.

8

When Liza went to meet the Clown at eight o'clock, she had a list in her pocket of things to talk about. There was so much they must remember if her plan was going to work.

He had not come when she got there. She waited, tense and nervous, watching the river road in the lingering sun. What if he never came? He could have decided it wasn't safe, or he could have simply changed his mind, or he could have been picked up by the KGB. She grew more and more apprehensive as the minutes passed. Then at seven minutes past eight by her watch, she saw him, coming along the street with his long steps, still carrying his old leather bag. She wondered what he had in the bag. She made herself look composed. Her father had once said, "Nobody gives me such a chill of fear as an excited person. I always expect disaster."

The Clown smiled at her broadly and sat down. "I was not so sure you come," he said.

She laughed. "I thought you weren't coming."

"How you have been?"

"Fine. And you?"

"Very good. No tragedy yet." He rolled the *r* in *tragedy* and looked skyward, mocking himself.

She was suddenly shy about telling him her plan. But it wouldn't do to put it off. Someone might notice them if they sat here too long.

While she hesitated, he took four small silver balls out of his pocket and began to juggle them. "You see, I practice. 'Never waste time,' they told us in school. 'Practice, practice, all the time practice.'" The silver balls flew up in the air faster and faster.

A woman walking by below them on the sidewalk looked up and saw him. For a moment she slowed her steps, watching. It frightened Liza. "It's very nice," she said, "but people notice. It attracts attention."

He looked suddenly downcast. He let the balls fall into his lap, and sat looking down at them. "To be alive attracts attention."

She couldn't stand it to see him sad. "I have a plan," she said, "to get you out of the country."

He looked at her, jerking his head as if she had literally shocked him. "I'm sorry? What did you say?"

"I think I know of a way to get you out of the country."

"That is impossible. I have no passport, no visa, nothing to leave the country."

73

"I know." She opened her purse and took out Uncle George's passport. Keeping it in her lap so she could hide it quickly if anyone came along, she opened it to the page with the picture. "Do you have any makeup?"

He stared at the passport. "Yes. In here." He touched his leather bag.

"I think you could pass for him, with a little work."

"But how is this? What happens to him?"

She told him the story quickly, Uncle George's vagueness, his mistake about the departure date, his engagement at the theater for Tuesday night. "I'll check out of both rooms and send the luggage down to the lobby. The Intourist car will take us to the airport. I'll meet you just outside the north entrance. I'll know the time tomorrow."

"But my English, it sounds Russian, does it not?"

She smiled. "A little. And anyway your English sounds English. Uncle George's is American. But we will do what we did in the taxi: you have a bad sore throat, laryngitis, you cannot speak. I will talk for you."

"What would happen to this man?" He touched the passport picture. "He would be arrested?"

She was glad he had thought of that. It made her like him all the more. "No. I spoke to a friend at the embassy. Not telling her anything, of course; it was just a general question. She said he should call the embassy and they will give him a temporary passport. And they'll get him on a plane home. He will be inconvenienced and very angry, but he won't be in any danger."

"But you. You would get in trouble."

"I don't think so. Just a routine scolding." She didn't say what she was thinking: "unless we're caught." She had thought about that quite thoroughly. She knew she could be, at best, imprisoned for several years for helping a citizen escape, taking the passport, and so on. The only answer she had for that was that they must not be caught. "The tickets are for Copenhagen. You could ask for asylum there. There would be no problem."

"I would not be returned?"

She realized that probably a Soviet citizen would never have heard that any of his fellow-citizens had defected to the West. "No. It has happened quite often. People get out somehow, or they are allowed to travel, like ballet and theater people, and then they go to the embassy in London or wherever they are, and ask for asylum. They always get it."

He thought for a long time. She waited impatiently. There was so much to talk about. They shouldn't waste a minute. Finally he shook his head. "You are very good, very kind. But I cannot do this."

Tears of disappointment filled her eyes. She hadn't dreamed he would say no. She had planned it so carefully. She turned her head away so he wouldn't see the tears, but he put his hand under her chin and turned her face toward him. There were tears in his eyes, too.

"You are afraid?" she said.

He answered her gently. "I am afraid for you. I myself, I am already doomed."

"But I have thought it all through. I want to do this."

"Why for me? You do not even know me."

"I do know you. I've watched you at the circus, again and again. I've talked to you. I know you. I've known you right from the beginning."

He looked at her thoughtfully. "It is a strange thing. I

75

feel that is true." He sighed. "But that is no reason for what happen to you if you help me and we are caught. The KGB, they are everywhere."

"But they wouldn't dream of your trying to leave the country this way." She wiped her eyes with her handkerchief, annoyed with herself for being so emotional when she should be calm. "Do you have a family?"

"No. No longer. There is no one to be hurt because of me."

"Except me," she said, "if you refuse to come." It was putting unfair pressure on him to say it that way, but it might work. And it was true enough. "I have no family either. The people I've loved are gone. I don't want you gone, too." And then, though she had had no intention of doing it, she told him about the deaths of her parents. He listened attentively, his expressive face full of sympathy and pain. When she had finished, he was again silent for several minutes.

"Very well," he said. "Tell me all the plan."

She went quickly into the details. They would meet somewhere again tomorrow to make sure everything was going all right. "Preferably not here. People might begin to notice."

"Perhaps outside the Lenin Library?" He smiled. "I am becoming very great authority on sea birds."

"Fine. Outside the library. Time?"

"Seventeen-thirty."

"Right." She was all business now. "I can't let you take the passport now because he might ask for it, for some reason, but study the face. I will bring, tomorrow, something of his for you to wear. Shirt and jacket. The trousers wouldn't fit, but be sure you cut out any Russian labels in your clothes. We must make you look as

American as possible. If you could lighten your hair a little . . ."

"Easily. And a little bald in front, yes?"

"Yes." She looked at her list. "You will carry Uncle George's suitcase. There's just one. Usually at customs here all they are interested in are books and letters. Uncle George is not a book man, and I'll take care of letters if there are any."

"Why books and letters?"

"They don't want tourists saying bad things about them, nor do they want us smuggling out manuscripts by Soviet authors, which has happened."

"Ah."

"Last year they read every page of my travel book that was about the Soviet Union. Well, anyway, what else?" She looked at the list again. "Make yourself look pale. Remember you have laryngitis." She touched her throat. "Very bad cold, chest and throat. I'll get some liniment so you'll smell authentic."

He laughed. "You think of everything."

"I've read a lot of spy novels."

A group of about fifteen Red Army soldiers strolled along the sidewalk. Liza watched them. "They make me nervous," she said. "There are so many of them everywhere."

He shrugged. "Russia has been attacked many times." He nodded toward University Hill. "From there Napoleon watched Moscow burn. Everyone, from the Vikings to Hitler, all attack. The Mongols, the Tartars, the Swedes, the Poles, the French, the Germans." He stared across the river with a brooding look. Then his face changed and he said, "But this is not time for history." He stood up. "Tomorrow at the library, yes?"

"All right. Be careful." As he walked off, it occurred to her that she didn't even know his name. In her excitement, she had lost the program he had signed when she had helped him last night. It made her sad. It was a souvenir she would have liked to keep.

In her room she made a list of things to remember. Get plane tickets from Intourist. Get clothes for Clown. Get one of Uncle George's caps to shade Clown's eyes. She worried about those brown eyes that ought to be blue. If she were really good at this business, she'd find some way to get him some contact lenses. But for all she knew, Russians might not even have contact lenses. Anyway she supposed they would have to be fitted to the person and probably signed for and all that. All she could do was hope that customs would be too busy making sure the visa was all right and so on, to examine the Clown's eyes. She thought of dark glasses, but they would attract attention; they would look as if he were hiding behind them. They'd just have to chance it.

She read her list over several times and added: Make sure he knows which entrance, and recheck time. Get rid of his leather bag, too old and foreign-looking. Tell him to leave or get rid of makeup, those silver balls, anything to do with circus. Find out if he has identity card and if so . . . . She tapped the paper with her pen. If so, what? Was it more dangerous to keep it or to get rid of it? It would be better if he had it in Copenhagen, but he must not be found with it at the border. She would get it from him and hide it somewhere on herself. It was very unlikely she would be searched except for her luggage and her purse. She'd think of some place to hide it.

She took her list into the bathroom, read it through

78

again, tore it up and flushed it down the toilet. Then, not trusting her memory, she made another one that no one would understand. 1. Tickets. 2. Coat, etc. 3. Uncle G's cap. 4. Bag. 5. Misc. 6. Id. No one would make much out of that.

Feeling restless and wanting to get away from the sensation of being monitored, she went down the hall to the TV room. A middle-aged American couple were the only people there. Liza sank down into one of the comfortable chairs, crossing her long legs. She stared at the screen not really thinking about what she saw, except now and then when it was loud enough to intrude on her attention. It was a documentary film about Cuba, and it was fiercely and sometimes crudely anti-American.

During a scene showing wealthy Americans drinking and gambling in what looked like an orgy, in pre-Castro Cuba, the American man began to mutter. Liza heard his wife try to shush him but he was getting angrier and angrier.

"Rotten propaganda," he said. "Nothing but rotten propaganda."

"Thomas, be quiet," his wife said.

There was a shot of American troops attacking people on the street in Central America a few minutes later and then a close-up shot of a Bank of America sign.

"See that?" the man exploded. "Lies! They're making it look like that's the official American bank. Just a bunch of lies."

Liza wished they would go away. She wanted to think. She could tune out the film, but it was harder to ignore the man, partly because she was concerned, as his wife was, that he would be overheard. Probably nothing would happen even if he was, but you never knew. That was what seemed most scary to her, that you really never knew what would happen. She remembered the man the embassy people had told them about last year, who had been picked up for bringing a copy of *Newsweek* magazine into the country at a time when the Soviet government was annoyed with *Newsweek*. He had been held for several days without even being able to ring up the embassy. Poor man, how bewildered and frightened he must have been. Her father had said, "Under circumstances like these, innocence becomes irrelevant."

She tried to remember everything that had taken place when she and her father went through customs on their way out, but she hadn't paid much attention then, and they had been traveling on a diplomatic passport, which undoubtedly made a difference.

The American wife prevailed upon her husband to leave. He would probably go home, Liza thought, and tell everyone that all Russians are liars. And people would believe him because, after all, he had been there. She wished somehow before she died that she could get even a handful of people to stop thinking of other people in categories: "All Russians are deceitful murdering criminals who want to destroy us, all Americans are loud-mouthed arrogant clods, all English people are hypocrites and snobs," and so on. Whole nations hated each other on the basis of myths like these.

She closed her eyes and tried to imagine the scene in the airport on Tuesday night. If she could just think in advance of everything that might happen, then she could be ready for it. But there were always things that never occurred to one at all until they happened. Those were the dangers. The only thing she could do was to keep cool and to keep her wits about her. Not panic, no matter what happened. And if the Clown got rattled, cover for him.

When she got up to leave the viewing room, she discovered that the documentary had ended and someone was playing the cello. Mademoiselle had told her she had very good powers of concentration. One must be careful, though, not to concentrate too hard sometimes, to keep one's attention open to everything.

She noticed when she picked up her key that Uncle George's was still there. She hoped he was enjoying the Praga. Poor Uncle George. She wished she could do him some big favor, to make up for all the trouble she was going to cause him. She wondered if he had had any word from Aunt May. She stopped in her tracks at a sudden thought: what if Aunt May called or wired him and mentioned his departure date? She went back to the desk and asked if there had been any messages for her or her uncle. The night clerk smiled at her and shook her head. Nothing.

It often took two or three hours to get served at a Moscow restaurant. Uncle George wouldn't be back for a long time. She picked up his key, saying to the girl at the desk that she wanted to check on his laundry. The girl gave it to her without hesitation.

She switched on Uncle George's lights and looked at the room with distaste. Partly for the sake of the monitor and partly because the untidiness got on her nerves, she picked up his things and put them in some kind of order. She opened the closet and took down one of his caps that was toward the back of the shelf. She thought it was a hideous cap, a blue, black, and white tattersall, but it looked like Uncle George. She pretended to find a spot on it, brushed at it, and then put the cap in her purse. She took the dark blue mackintosh off its hanger, looked it over, and hung it over her arm. If Uncle George looked for it, she could say she'd sent it down to be cleaned.

She opened his drawers and straightened things up a bit. She took out a lightweight blue turtleneck jersey. Maybe all these blues would make the Clown's eyes look blue, like a chameleon. At least he would look like an American. She hoped it wouldn't be too warm an evening for him to wear the mac.

She decided to leave Uncle George a note. She sat down at the desk and opened the drawer to find some paper. Russian hotels didn't provide stationery, but there was half a pad of air mail paper that Aunt May had probably left.

Dear Uncle George:
I picked up your room a bit. Hope you don't mind. Hope you enjoyed the Praga. I'll get you tickets for Teatr Mimiki in the morning and leave them on your desk. Don't worry about packing. I'll take care of it.

Liza

She felt like a miserable hypocrite, making herself sound so helpful when all the time it was a plot. She had to keep telling herself what the stakes were.

As she started to close the drawer, she saw an official-looking piece of paper. She picked it up. The customs declaration! She had completely forgotten about that. When they left the country, they had to turn it back in. She put it in her pocket, closed the door, and returned Uncle George's key to the desk.

In her own room she went into the bathroom and looked at Uncle George's customs declaration. He had declared a hundred dollars in traveler's checks, $260 in U.S. cash, and a gold wristwatch. Although it was not asked for, he had also written in "two cameras." She folded the slip and put it inside his passport. It shook her that she had forgotten anything so important as the customs declaration. There would have been a terrible fuss if the Clown had not been able to produce one. She sat down and put her head on her hands, trying to think if there was anything else like that she had overlooked. What a lot of things lawbreakers had to worry about!

To her list she added "camera" and "watch" and "cash." With luck she might be able to take one of Uncle George's cameras, unless he took both of them to the theater. If customs asked, she could say that Aunt May had taken the cameras with her, although it seemed like a pretty unlikely story. But it wasn't usually things like cameras the customs people were interested in. You couldn't be sure, though, because all customs were unpredictable. Sometimes, not in Russia of course but in other countries, you could sail right through without anything but a quick glance at your passport and a stamp, and other times everything was looked at.

For a minute she felt a surge of hot panic, thinking about what might happen to her and to the Clown if they were caught. Then she pulled herself together and dismissed the thought. They simply must not be caught.

9

In the morning she left Uncle George's list for the day under his door. After her breakfast she reserved two tickets for him at the Teatr Mimiki for Tuesday evening, and on impulse she got him a pair of seats for the Kremlin Theater for Monday evening. Then she went over to the travel desk in the big Intourist office to get the plane tickets back.

The young woman at the desk was reading *Pravda*. For several minutes she didn't look up. Then she glanced at Liza, ignored her, and began to talk to the woman at the voucher desk. Liza waited patiently at first, but then she began to get annoyed. This had happened to her before with Intourist people. Sometimes they were very nice and helpful, but some of them, like this one, went out of the way to be rude.

"I'd like to pick up my plane tickets," Liza said finally.

The young woman looked at her with a wide-eyed, challenging stare. She was quite pretty, with vivid blue eyes and dark hair. "Sit down," she said.

Liza sat down and was sorry at once that she had. Sitting down put one at a disadvantage. One was turned into a supplicant. The woman resumed her conversation with the person at the next desk. She talked rapidly in Russian and they laughed a good deal. They talked so fast, Liza couldn't follow them, but she knew they were making fun of her. She caught isolated words, "English," "tourist," "stupid."

She leaned forward. "The names are Asher and Parke. George Asher and Liza Parke. For Copenhagen tomorrow night."

Again she got the wide-eyed, mocking stare. "Come back at two o'clock."

Liza stood up. "I was told to come this morning."

"They're not ready." The woman picked up her newspaper.

Liza smiled sweetly. "You haven't looked."

The woman's eyes flashed with anger. "Come back at two o'clock."

Liza leaned against the desk, and the Intourist woman shrank back a little, as if her territory had been invaded. Liza picked up a crystal paperweight and moved it an inch. "Would you look and make sure? I shall be busy at two o'clock." She spoke in a low, reasonable voice.

There was a long pause. Then the woman jerked open a drawer in her desk, flipped through a file, and brought out the tickets. She threw them across the desk toward Liza and she said, "Come here at twenty hours tomorrow night to get the number of your car." She

85

tipped back her head and glared at Liza, but there was a new look there, too, and Liza recognized it. She had learned in her first years of boarding school that if you refused to let yourself be bullied, the bully would give up. Some of her friends were people who had started out trying to push her around when she was a new girl.

She thanked the woman and went over to the bank window to change all but a couple of rubles back into Danish currency. She had to give the bank clerk the form that she'd been given when she came into the country and had cashed some of her traveler's checks for rubles. The Clown would not be able to take any money out with him. She must remember to give him some American bills to put in his pocket. She always carried some in her passport case. She wondered if it would upset him not to be able to take any money. She could lend him all he needed, but sometimes people were funny about that, especially men. She hadn't really thought about what would happen after he got to Denmark, and she decided not to burden herself with that now. There was enough to think of.

She went around to the foreign currency shop and bought a man's gold wristwatch of Swiss make. The one she chose was not, she was sure, a watch that Uncle George would have chosen. It was a simple gold rectangle, slightly curved to fit the wrist. It would look lovely on the Clown and she liked the feeling of buying him a present. Her practical mind noticed, however, how much more the price was than it would have been in Zurich.

She bought a jar of caviar for Walter and a filmy pale green scarf for Harriet. She looked all over the big shop for something suitable for Mademoiselle, but she could never make up her mind. It should be in very good taste, beautiful, but not expensive enough to distress Mademoiselle. In the end she didn't buy anything.

She took her purchases up to her room and slipped the Kremlin Theater tickets under Uncle George's door with a note explaining what and when they were for and telling him she would leave the Teatr Mimiki tickets in the morning. If she gave them to him now, he'd probably lose them or go to the theater on the wrong night.

In the middle of the afternoon she went to the Tretyakov Gallery to see the large collection of icons. There were all kinds from all over Russia, dating from the eleventh century. Many of them were made of beaten gold, the faces done in mosaic, sometimes lapis lazuli. The early ones were in low relief but later ones were almost three-dimensional with the faces set back against the frame. Some were painted wood, the paint often faded or chipped off. She remembered reading in Aline Mosby's book on Russia that if you found a wooden icon in an antique shop, you should touch the back of it with a lighted match to lure out and kill the bugs in the old wood. Were they woodworms? She couldn't remember. Well, worms had to live somewhere.

She stood for a long time looking at a beautiful thin gold chalice with the figures of Christ and eleven apostles in high relief. Poor Judas, he got left out. She had always felt sorry for Judas. She looked so long at the chalice, she realized finally that the custodian was watching her. She moved away, thinking what a lovely present for Mademoiselle the chalice would have been. It was a pity that all the beautiful art the churches and the royalty had produced would never be made any more. It was probably wicked to have beaten-gold icons and fabulous jeweled crowns and palaces with golden walls when peasants went hungry, and yet it brought beauty to people for hundreds of years.

She left enough time to take a shower and change her clothes before she went to meet the Clown. She looked over her dresses, not quite satisfied with any of them. Finally she chose a featherweight white Irish tweed trousersuit that she had bought when she spent the holidays with her friend Mackie in Dublin.

She folded up Uncle George's blue turtleneck sweater and the mackintosh and put them in the big plastic shopping bag that Aunt May had left behind. The gold watch went into her purse. She almost forgot Uncle George's cap. It went on top of the other things. Then she consulted her list. Nothing else that she had to take to him now. He would have to wear his own trousers because Uncle George wasn't as tall, and he was quite a lot bigger around the waist. She would remind the Clown again to remove any Russian labels. It seemed very unlikely that he would be searched with any such thoroughness, but if he were, there should be nothing to give him away. If they questioned him, well, if they questioned him with any persistence, they were sunk. That laryngitis business would only go so far. But if she were careful and thought of everything, there wouldn't be anything to make them suspicious. The responsibility, as the time of leaving came closer, made her shiver.

Because she was a little early, she walked slowly toward the Lenin State Library, pushing her way through the crowds hurrying home from work. The sky was cloudy, and the air a little cooler than it had been. She hoped it would be like this tomorrow night so it would seem natural for the Clown to be wearing the mackintosh. Of course he could carry it if necessary, but the coat would give him a little extra bulk.

She walked past the library entrance and slowly back again, watching the door. At exactly 5:30 she saw him. He was in a group of people and was wearing glasses, which made him look a little different. He stopped on the step and took off his glasses, looking for her. She waved. He ran down the steps toward her and stood smiling down at her, putting his glasses away in a case in his pocket.

"Could you wear those tomorrow night?" she said.

"The glasses? I wear to read. Yes, I could wear them."

"They might disguise your eyes a little, the color of them, I mean. Especially if you let the glasses get a little streaky. You know, dirty."

"Yes, of course. I have the wrong color eyes, yes." He took her arm and they walked up the street. "Shall we take the Metro?"

"All right."

As they walked he said, "Would you like to know about the puffin?" He tapped the notebook in his pocket.

She laughed. She felt very happy. "I'd love to know about the puffin."

"It is of the family auk. Do you say like 'awk' or 'owk?' "

" 'Awk,' I think."

"Yes. Found along British coast. Very good to swim

and dive. Black and white feathers with nose like a parrot and orange feet. Very friendly birds with each other. Like communists. Large colonies together, even thousands."

"That's very interesting," Liza said. "I never really knew about puffins." She loved the shine in his eyes when he was amused.

"The mother, before the egg, she digs into a cliff and stays underground for six weeks until egg comes. One egg."

"It must get terribly dreary underground."

He laughed. "Oh, but the beautiful egg. Very white and fine." He lifted his hand. "And that is all I know about the puffin."

"I'm very glad to know all that." It was nice to walk with someone as tall as the Clown. She was taller than most of the boys her age, and it was awkward when they had to look up to her.

He led her down the long flight of stairs to the underground, holding her arm as they pushed through the crowd and boarded a train. She sat sideways in order to look out the window at the handsome murals in the stations. The Clown stood in front of her, holding to a strap. They didn't talk because of the crowd, but when she caught his eye, he smiled and lifted one eyebrow in a quizzical way. She had always wished she could lift one eyebrow like that. She had practiced in front of a mirror, but when one went up, the other went up, too. She decided it must be a gift, like a good singing voice or the ability to write poetry.

They rode a long way, the people getting off at the various stops along the route until there were only a dozen or so left on the train. The Clown stooped to look out at a station sign, nodded to her, and took her arm to guide her off the train.

When they came out above ground, they were in a residential suburb with blocks and blocks of identical high-rise apartment houses. Liza noted the name of the station and kept track of the streets as the Clown, who seemed familiar with the neighborhood, guided her down a small hill to a park. At that hour the park was almost empty. They sat down on a bench under a huge tree. There were brightly blooming beds of flowers laid out along the paths, carefully tended.

"Pretty," Liza said.

"No ears to hear." He nodded vaguely toward the west. "My friend's apartment is over there."

"I see." She put the shopping bag on the bench. "I brought you some things to wear tomorrow night, so you will look American."

"Ah, very good."

"I think they'll fit. You will remember to take out any Russian labels in your things?"

"I remember. Last night, very late, I practice makeup to look like the American uncle."

"Oh. How was it?"

"Good. I remember his face well, you see, because I drew him. I think I will look enough like."

Liza showed him the customs declaration. She explained about the money exchange. The Clown was distressed at not being able to take out any money.

"I had not thought of that. No money. That is bad. What will I do?"

"You can stay with us until you get settled. Or forever if you like." She took a hundred dollars in American cash from her wallet. "Keep this in your pocket. They will ask to see what money you have. You won't be able to have any rubles, so there's no problem about exchange." As she had expected, he was reluctant to take the money. "No, you must. It would look odd to have no money with you. Don't worry; it's just a loan if that makes you feel better."

He looked at it curiously. "I never saw American money. It is nice. Who is this man?"

"George Washington. The first president. Why don't you try on the mackintosh and the cap? There's no one here. We'll see if they fit."

Obediently he took them out of the bag. "Very nice," he said, holding up the coat. He stood up and put it on. It was a little big in the shoulders but not bad.

"You look very nice," Liza said. "Try the cap."

She laughed when he put it on squarely in the center of his head, the way Scandinavians wore their caps. "You look more like a Dane than an American. Uncle George tilts it just a bit."

"Tilts?"

She got up and adjusted it for him. Then she sat down again quickly, embarrassed at the intimacy. She began to talk fast to cover her confusion.

"I'll keep the customs declaration with the passport. Oh, and you had better not bring your leather bag. It looks very Russian."

He nodded. He was looking down at the raincoat, patting the pockets, adjusting the belt, like a child with a new coat. She wasn't sure he was listening.

"And whatever you have in the bag—remember,

they will go through your luggage probably quite thoroughly."

"I will leave everything. It is my makeup, my props."

"Oh." It was sad to have to leave those. "I'm sorry."

He shrugged. "Easy to make more. The glasses, the hat."

"And the little silver balls."

He sighed. "Those I will miss."

She thought a minute. "Why don't you give them to me? They wouldn't look suspicious if I had them."

"No. I can get more. No use to take chance."

"Do you have an I.D. card?"

He readjusted his cap at a different angle. It made him look very jaunty. "Sorry?"

"Identity card? Like a passport for inside Russia?"

"Oh. Yes." He showed her the small red passport.

"Keep it until we're ready to get into the car, or perhaps until we are in the car. Then give it to me. I will hide it. It mustn't be on you anywhere."

"You will hide it well?" He looked worried. "That is the most dangerous of all."

It occurred to her right then what she would do with it. "I have a beret . . ." She pointed to his cap. "A cap, sort of. I'll slit the lining and slip it in there, and I'll wear the beret." She was pleased with herself for thinking of such a brilliant idea, but he still seemed worried.

"It would not be better to destroy?"

"I think it would be good for you to have it in Copenhagen. It proves who you are. Officials worry if you don't have any identification. Don't worry, it will be safe. They never search one's hat."

She had put off giving him the watch because she felt shy about it. It was like giving him a present, and she wasn't sure how he'd react. But it had to be done. She got the flat box out of her purse.

"On Uncle George's customs declaration he declared a gold watch." She handed him the box. "I thought you'd better have one."

He opened the box and caught his breath. "It is very fine watch."

"Oh, not really. I got it at the shop for tourists, where the prices are low." She crossed her fingers, thinking "not all that low."

He looked at it without taking it out of the box. "It is necessary to have a watch?"

"Yes. They sometimes check to see if you're taking out what you brought in. In case you might have sold to the black market people, which is very illegal."

"I see."

She was feeling more and more nervous. She was afraid she had been tactless. But it was true, they might check, and if he couldn't produce a gold watch, he'd be in trouble. "We can sell it when we get to Copenhagen if you don't want to keep it."

He looked at her quickly. "It is very beautiful. I like it very much. It is just that you do so much . . ." He brightened. "I buy it from you when I am again working."

"All right. Fine."

He took it out of the box and tried it on. He held out his wrist for her to see, his misgivings gone. "Beautiful!"

"It does look nice." She was glad it fitted. He had slender wrists.

94

"I am very splendid American!" He jumped up and capered around the bench, doing a tricky little dance step. Two small boys who were chasing each other nearby stopped to look at him. They came closer when he leaped lightly over the bench as if it were nothing but a small hurdle.

Liza looked around but there was no one else in sight. She was charmed by his exuberance but also she worried that someone might notice him and become curious. It was not after all usual for a grown man to caper about and fly over benches. Now he swooped down on the startled boys and caught their hands.

"Round and round!" He pulled them in a circle, faster and faster. After a moment they responded delightedly. The three of them whirled. The Clown held out a hand to Liza, but she laughed and shook her head. She could never do things like that no matter how much she would like to. She was always the one, on travels, who watched the fiesta crowds from a balcony and stayed a little way off from celebrations. "Inhibited," her friends said, but she couldn't help it. She enjoyed watching other people let themselves go like that, but she couldn't do it herself.

The Clown lined up the boys and leap-frogged over them and back again. Then he did a magnificent series of cartwheels. The children, who were six or seven and who looked alike, were laughing with excitement.

The older one said to the Clown, "What is your name?"

The Clown drew himself up tall, puffed out his cheeks and made his eyelids droop. "My name is George Washington."

Liza burst out laughing. Somehow, unlikely as it seemed, he had caught the expression of the face on the dollar bill. She jumped at the sound of a voice, but it was only the boys' nanny calling them. She came toward them, flapping her apron as if they were chickens. She was an elderly, pleasant-looking babushka.

"Come, come, come," she said. "Your mama wants you."

The older boy said, "Nina Federovna, this is Mr. Washington."

She bowed. "Good evening, Mr. Washington."

He swept off his cap and returned the bow. "Madame. Good evening."

She gathered up the boys and hustled them off toward one of the apartment houses. The Clown sat down beside Liza, not even out of breath. He laughed. "Do not worry. I will not do this on airplane."

She shook her head. He was disconcertingly quick to read her thoughts. "I enjoyed it."

He leaned back and stretched out his long legs. "Would you perhaps tell me if you can all that may happen tomorrow night? We take taxi to airport?"

It was a quick change of mood. It took her a moment to gather her thoughts. "No, not a taxi, an Intourist car. In the hotel they will tell me the number of the car and it will be there at 8:00. The entrance where we came in in the taxi, you remember?"

He nodded. "The north, off Razin Street."

"Yes. You must be prompt because they get annoyed if one keeps them waiting."

He made a face. "We will not keep them waiting."

96

"I'm not sure if it is always exactly the same, but he will probably drive us around in back of the airport to one of the rooms where Intourist is. They will examine our luggage, probably quite thoroughly. They will ask to see any money you have. They will go through my purse and your wallet. They will ask if we have rubles. They will take our passports and remove the visas. Then the Intourist person will take us out to the plane and see that we get on."

"They leave no loops."

"No loopholes. No, they don't. They make quite sure one is on his way out."

"Loop . . . holes." He practiced it once or twice. "I must improve the English."

"You speak very good English. I wish I spoke Russian as well."

"I like language. I study French and English in school."

"Oh, that's good that you speak French. If there is any kind of real problem where you have to speak to me in front of other people, speak in French, all right? I think they'd be less likely to notice your Russian accent."

"Very well." He rolled up Uncle George's sweater and put it under his arm and gave her back the shopping bag. "I take you back now."

"I can go alone."

"No, I take you to your station."

"All right." It was nice to be looked after.

On the train she went over everything in her mind to make sure she had not forgotten anything. There would be no further chance to talk.

He left her at the station near the hotel. "Do not worry, I will be on time." He looked at his new watch.

At the top of the stairs, she looked back. He was still there, watching her.

10

Liza slept badly. She kept waking up with a start trying to remember if there was anything she had overlooked. Toward morning she did think of something. There was a second lobby directly below the main lobby. What if the Intourist cars left from there? She couldn't remember seeing luggage piled up in the main lobby. She would have to check in the morning to see. If the car did leave from the lower level, she would have to dash upstairs and find the Clown, who would be at the main level. Oh, dear. Her head ached. She pulled the thin blanket up and shivered. She had to keep steady. She almost wished she had one of those little tranquilizers her roommate took whenever she felt nervous. But Liza had never taken one, and she was afraid it might make her less alert. She was going to have to be more alert than she had ever been in her life. She must foresee and if possible forestall any problem that might come up.

She had heard Uncle George come in around midnight, probably from the Kremlin Theater. She hoped things were going well so he wouldn't get temperamental and decide not to follow his schedule.

She got up just as the sky turned light gray and began to pack. She would have to pack some of Uncle George's things quickly at the last possible moment, after he had left for the Teatr Mimiki. If he changed his mind about going to the theater, what then? It was a horrifying thought. But he was unlikely to spend his last night in Moscow hanging around the hotel room. She packed carefully and methodically. On top of her clothes she put her Russian guidebook, her Berlitz phrase book, and the copy of *Persuasion*. She was pretty sure they would look those over carefully, and perhaps that would take attention away from the Clown. She had noticed when they came in that the customs men had given so much time to going through her books and a couple of letters that she had not had time to mail, that they gave only a brief glance at Aunt May's and Uncle George's luggage.

With her manicure scissors she snipped some stitches that attached the lining to the cloth of her beret, just enough so she would be able to slip in the little red identity card. She put a small safety pin in her wallet so she could pin the lining back into place. She was still rather pleased with herself about that idea.

She made up Uncle George's last list, clipped the

voucher for the theater tickets to the list, wrote a note reminding him what time the play started and that he must give the voucher to the box office to get his tickets, gave him the name of Meredith's friend again, reminded him that he had an appointment with his actor friend. She thought a minute. Then she added, "In case you want to take him or anybody else to dinner, I'll make an early reservation . . ." Then she tore up the note and wrote it again, leaving out the last sentence. She had been going to say she'd make him a reservation for dinner, but if the theater curtain was at 7:30, he wouldn't have time to get served. Instead she told him she would reserve a late dinner table for him at Aragvi after the show. That would keep him away from the hotel until about midnight at the earliest. By that time, God willing, she and the Clown would be in Copenhagen. She wrote herself a memo to call Aragvi.

When it was late enough not to disturb other people with the loud plumbing, she took a long bath and washed her hair. She had planned to eat breakfast early, but the idea of eating made her feel ill. She'd wait.

She heard the whir of the telephone ringing in Uncle George's room. She tensed. It could be the desk calling to wake him. It could be Intourist for some reason or other, or Aunt May, or Meredith's friend saying he couldn't make it tonight. She leaned against the wall to listen.

The phone rang again and Uncle George answered, sleepy and annoyed. "Yes?" he said in the loud voice he used for people who didn't speak English. "Hello? What is it? Is this the desk? I can't understand a word you're saying. You have the wrong number."

Liza heard him slam down the phone, muttering. It rang again.

"Hello? Hello? You have the wrong number. I don't know what you're talking about. I don't speak your lingo." He hung up again.

It kept on ringing, but he didn't answer it again. She heard him banging around in the room, heard the water running in the shower. She decided to wait and give Uncle George his list and his tickets instead of slipping them under the door. It would relieve some of the suspense to find out whether he had changed his plans or anything. She added a memo to the list, giving him Meredith's office and home phone numbers "in case you need them." She must be quite sure he had those, so he could call her when he got stranded. She wondered what Meredith would think. It would probably be the middle of the night when he called because that was when he would get home to find he had been checked out of the hotel. Actually, she thought, as far as money goes, he was entitled to spend the night in his room. They had had to give an extra day's voucher because they would be occupying the rooms past the noon checkout time. But Intourist would probably not see it that way. They would only see that he was supposed to be gone and he wasn't. Poor Uncle George. She really was sorry. Now that she was doing him such a disservice, he didn't irritate her any more. He just seemed pathetic.

She opened her door a little so she would be sure to see him when he went out. The day was cool and cloudy. She would have to be prepared for his asking about his mac.

She waited nervously for him to come. It seemed to take him forever. No wonder Aunt May always complained about how slow he was. But at last she heard him open his door. She went to her own door and waited while he struggled with the big key in the lock.

"Good morning," she said.

"Oh, Liza. Do you know where in thunder my raincoat is? I can't believe May would take it with her, although she took my favorite sweater . . ."

"I sent it to be cleaned, Uncle George."

He growled. "What'd you do that for? It wasn't dirty."

"The sleeve was dirty."

"Oh. Well, what do I do if it pours? Get soaked, I suppose."

"I could lend you my brolly."

"Your what?"

"Sorry. My umbrella."

"You've got to be kidding. Me carry an umbrella? What do you think I am?"

"European men carry umbrellas."

"Well, I'm not a European. I guess I'll just have to get wet."

"Take taxis," Liza said, trying to sound calm and reasonable. "You won't get wet."

"You women," he grumbled. "Always messing around with a man's things." He settled his shoulders into his jacket as if it were already raining. "You got my list?"

"Yes." She gave it to him. "And this is the slip for the theater tickets for tonight. I've made you a reservation for two after the show at the Aragvi."

"How did you happen to do that?" He looked suspicious.

"I thought you might be hungry. It's so hard to get anything to eat during intermission."

"You can say that again. It's a madhouse. At the Kremlin last night I nearly got trampled to death."

"Oh, you went to the Kremlin Theater, did you?"

He looked surprised. "Naturally. You didn't think I'd waste those tickets?"

She felt relieved. "No, of course not. Did you have someone to go with you?"

"Yeah, that movie actor fellow. He's a nice guy."

"Maybe he can go with you tonight."

"Sure. He's going to take me on the set today. I'll get some pictures."

She noticed that he had only one of his two cameras with him.

"You won't be back till late then." It was a rather risky question if only because it wasn't the kind of thing she would normally ask him, but she had to know.

He didn't seem to think it odd. "No, I don't think so. It's kind of a tight schedule. He's asked me over to his place for tea or some darned thing."

"Oh, that's lovely." Thank heaven for the Russian film actor, whoever he was. Of course he might be KGB. She knew they sometimes kept track of tourists, and a tourist so bent on taking pictures might arouse interest. If he was KGB, he would know that Uncle George was due to leave tonight. If this were only a reasonable country where all this suspicion didn't exist. But if it were, of course, there wouldn't have been any problem about the Clown in the first place. She would have to hope that the film actor was just a film actor, probably enjoying cadging a few free meals from the rich American.

104

"Well, see you." Uncle George started down the hall. "You'll pack my junk, right?"

"Yes."

"Okay."

The phone in his room began to ring again. Liza held her breath.

Uncle George hesitated. "Those idiots! They've been ringing wrong numbers all morning. I can't get anything through their heads." The phone rang again.

"I'll take care of it," Liza said.

He tossed her the key and left. By the time Liza had unlocked the door and gone into Uncle George's room, the phone had stopped ringing. The room was in as much of a mess as if she had not cleaned it the day before. Well, she'd start packing his things, leaving a few things, like pajamas and robe and his Dopp-Kit, until the last minute, just in case he did decide to come back to the room before eight o'clock.

Her own phone began to ring. She went back to her room and answered it. A long-distance operator confirmed her name and asked her to hold on. After a long wait, she heard Aunt May's voice, faint and with that echo that long-distance connections sometimes make.

"Aunt May?"

"Liza. Is that you?"

"Yes." Aunt May always asked the obvious. But what luck that she had missed Uncle George. Liza could hardly keep her voice steady.

"I've been trying to get George," Aunt May said. "He kept hanging up."

"He thought it was a wrong number."

"Is he there?"

"No, he's gone out."

"Oh, what rotten luck. Well, it's nothing vital. Everything is all right?"

"Fine. He's getting some pictures."

"Good. I can't talk long. It costs a fortune. Just tell him things are working out fine here. He'll know what I mean."

"I'll tell him."

"Be sure he gets to the airport."

"All right, Aunt May."

" 'Bye, dear."

Liza sat with her hand on the phone, thinking. If everything was "working out fine," that meant Aunt May had not been cut out of her father's will. That would make Uncle George happy. And maybe they wouldn't try to get Liza to stay with them. They would be angry, of course, after she tricked Uncle George, but anyway they wouldn't be so interested in what they thought was her "fortune." She didn't hold it against them that they were so concerned with money. It was just the way they were. Walter had told her once that only people who had never been without money could afford to be casual about it.

She went back to the other room and began to pack Uncle George's bag. It would be nice if she could get the message to him about Aunt May's money. That would put him in a good mood. She began to think about how she was going to get his passport, ticket, and suitcase back to him. If he caught a plane out tomorrow morning, he would still make the New York connection. His things could be left at the airline passenger desk in Copenhagen. If only she could leave him a note here at the floor desk telling him to call Meredith, but the

Russians would read it, and in fact probably throw it away because they would think he had gone. She felt suddenly extremely angry with the Russians. Why did they have to make everything so difficult? And what a lot of unnecessary work they made for themselves. She thought of all those people on the twenty-first floor monitoring thousands of tourists day and night. What a boring, tedious, squalid job! "And what is your profession, Igor?" "I am Peeping Tom number 2,106, for Mother Russia." Ugh!

She packed everything except Uncle George's pajamas, robe, slippers, and toilet things. There were five rolls of exposed film. She hoped they wouldn't make a fuss about that. But certainly most tourists took unprocessed film out with them. His other camera, a Yashica, was in its case. The Clown could wear that over his shoulder, a sure sign of a tourist, although they were more likely to have Instamatics than Yashicas. She wondered what had happened to the sketch the Clown had made of Uncle George. Probably Aunt May had taken it home, or perhaps Uncle George had thrown it away. It wasn't a cruel sketch, but it was not exactly flattering either.

Among Uncle George's things she found a small tube of Vicks Vaporub. She put it in her pocket to give the Clown. He would smell like a real, true Yankee with a cold.

She remembered to call the Aragvi and make an after-theater reservation for Uncle George. It was still early. She would have to find something absorbing to do or she would go mad. She felt terribly nervous.

Down in the lobby she found a small group of tourists

about to leave for a tour of the Kremlin. She hated guided tours, but it was something to do and there were things she wanted to see in the Kremlin. She found one of her unused tour coupons and joined the group.

The guide was a student, a pale thin girl who seemed to feel considerable disdain for her group, especially for two plump little middle-aged couples from New York, who asked a lot of questions. But they were intelligent questions, and the guide became after a while a little less superior. One of the men, who had a strong European accent, told Liza he taught history at New York University. She began to listen more to him than to the guide. In the Armory Museum he pointed out to her the ancient Cap of Monomakh that Ivan III had used to crown his grandson in 1498, and he showed her Ivan the Terrible's mail armor. He and his wife and Liza lingered so long to admire Boris Godunov's jeweled ring that the guide grew impatient. They saw the enormous boots of Peter the Great.

"Think of a kick in the pants from that foot, eh?" the little professor said, while his wife pretended to be shocked by him.

"Be serious, Nathan," she said, "be serious."

They stood in front of Boris Godunov's throne while the guide reeled off statistics about its weight, the number of serfs probably required to build it, and so on. She spoke of the past with a curious mixture of proprietary pride and contempt, and leveled a cool look at Liza when she pointed out a set of English Renaissance silver, which, she said, was better than any to be found in the British Empire.

They walked over to the bell tower and listened dutifully while she recited the number of large bells and small chimes in the carillon, and told a wan little joke about the nearly twelve-ton "chip" that broke off when the bell fell from its scaffolding in the mid-eighteenth century. The professor made a joke of his own, which Liza didn't get, but she laughed anyway because he was a nice little man and she didn't like his being snubbed by the guide.

When she got back to the hotel, Liza remembered she hadn't had any breakfast. It was early for lunch, but she climbed the stairs at the end of the wing looking for a buffet that was open. When she finally found one, she had a sausage, some bread, and some cool *limonada*. Then only the afternoon lay before her. She wondered what the Clown was doing.

11

Later there were long stretches of that afternoon that she couldn't remember at all. She took a long walk and began to think in vivid images of all the stories, real or rumored, that she had ever heard about people who had been arrested in Russia. She remembered a scary documentary she had seen once on the BBC about the secret police in the Soviet Union. It wasn't clear though whether she was remembering it accurately or whether it was all mixed up in her mind with her own fears and the stories she had heard. She imagined the Clown arrested, questioned mercilessly under a blinding overhead light, kept in solitary confinement, sent off to an unknown place of horror in Siberia or some terrible hospital for the insane. She saw herself on trial. There would be a fuss because she was an American, but she knew quite well that if she broke the law in a foreign country, there was nothing her own country could do for her. She pictured herself in some prison, alone, ill-fed, unable to communicate.

She got so worked up, she was almost ready to renounce the whole plan, both for the Clown's sake and for her own. But then she reminded herself that all these awful things and worse would certainly happen to the Clown if he stayed in Russia. He was already hunted, and by now he had deserted the circus troupe, which to the police would mark him as guilty of something. He would be arrested and convicted as soon as the KGB caught up with him. They would remember his brother.

She found herself at last in another one of Moscow's many attractive little parks. She sat down near a group of children and tried to pull herself together. Her hands were trembling and she felt nauseated. This would never do. She had made her decision. 'Never look back, Liza,' she told herself sternly.

One of the younger children, a boy about three years old, tossed his ball at her suddenly. Surprised, she caught it and tossed it back. He laughed and threw it again. For several minutes she was involved in a game of catch with him. Then he ran off to play with his friends. His babushka, on the next bench, nodded and smiled approvingly at Liza and called something that Liza didn't catch. The scene was so normal, so pleasant, Liza felt reassured and some of the nightmare visions faded. Later, in some of the moments of greatest tension, the image of that laughing little boy flashed across her mind and helped her to stay calm.

When it began to rain, she found herself standing near a bridge that crossed the broad river. She looked at her watch. It was time to be getting back to the hotel. She'd better eat something, even though the idea of food made her stomach tighten.

She found a small café where at that time of the afternoon there were no customers except three workmen, two of them drinking tea, and the other drinking the thick clabbered milk that Russians seemed to enjoy. She tried not to look at the milk as she ordered some tea and pointed out a kind of meat pie to the girl behind the counter. It was hot and good.

A steady summer rain was ruffling the surface of the gray river when she came out. She waved down a cab although she felt like walking in the rain. It wouldn't do to get her clothes soaking wet, since she would have to wear them until late that night. She couldn't remember what time they would get to Copenhagen. The flight would probably take three or four hours. She tried to think how long it had taken coming over, but she hadn't paid much attention.

It was a relief to find Uncle George's key still at the desk. Irina stopped her in the corridor to say good-bye. Liza wished she had thought to get her some little present. She knew Irina would refuse a tip.

"Take care of yourself," Irina said, hugging her. "Be a good girl."

"I will, Irina. You take care of yourself, too."

"Oh, yes. I do that." She nodded at Uncle George's room. "He will be back, your uncle? He is not all packed."

"I'll pack for him. He's going to meet me downstairs when it's time to go to the airport."

Irina looked disapproving. "You have to do everything?"

Liza said, "Oh, I'm used to travel. I like to do it." She wanted to get Irina's mind off Uncle George. On an impulse she took three rubles from her purse and said, "Irina, will you buy something for your little girl?"

"No, no, no," Irina said, patting Liza's hand, but she followed her into the room and stepped into the bathroom. She smiled at Liza, but for a moment Liza didn't understand. Then she realized what Irina meant. She would like to have the money for her little girl, but she didn't want "them" to see her taking it. Liza went into the bathroom and put the money in Irina's hand. In a second Irina had put it in her big pocket, had given Liza a quick kiss on the cheek, and stepped out of the bathroom with a couple of towels over her arm. Liza had thought of the one way to get Irina to accept money; she was glad.

She wished Irina would stay and talk to her, but of course she had her work to do. They said good-bye again, and Irina walked down the long hall with her scurrying mouselike gait. Liza watched her go, feeling sad that she would never see her again. One was always getting to know nice people and never seeing them again.

At 6:30 she finished packing Uncle George's suitcase and shut it, keeping the key in her wallet. She didn't want the Clown to have to struggle with the unfamiliar lock. She took the suitcase and the camera into her room and then went back to make sure she hadn't overlooked anything. She checked her own room. To fill up time she wrote a letter to her friend in Dublin, a newsy, touristy letter, telling her about the things in the museums, the icons, and so on. She didn't mention the circus. She put the letter, sealed and addressed, on top of her clothes in the suitcase. She was pretty sure customs would rip it open and read it, and anything she could do to keep attention focused on herself and away from the Clown was advantage gained.

She went downstairs at seven o'clock to get her check-out slip at the reception desk. It took longer than she had expected. It always struck her as unreasonable that people like the woman who sold postcards or the woman who had the little table where aspirin and such things were sold, should speak quite good English, whereas the women behind the reception desk, whom one really needed to communicate with, spoke no English at all. She made several attempts in her uncertain Russian to make the clerk understand that she was checking out Uncle George as well as herself. She got quite nervous and couldn't remember words in Russian that she knew perfectly well. Finally a young woman, a Russian, who was standing nearby, offered to interpret, and the whole matter was straightened out.

Liza asked one of the porters to come up and get the bags. She was doing all this early because you never knew what delays might come up. As she was turning away, she remembered about the two levels. She came back and asked him which level the Intourist cars left from. He pointed down. She would have to wait upstairs for the Clown then, and whisk him down quickly when he came. They might be a minute or two late, but there was no danger of the car going without them, she was sure. She was glad she had thought of it. How awful if they had been waiting for each other on different levels.

As Liza had expected, it took the porter ten or fifteen minutes to come up for the bags. Then there was a delay while the floor clerk came in and counted the towels, the glasses, the ashtrays, everything movable, checking them off on her list before the porter was allowed to remove Liza's luggage. Uncle George's room had to be checked out, too. For a minute the clerk couldn't find one of the ashtrays, and Liza was afraid he might have taken it, although she hadn't seen it in his things. Finally it was found on the floor behind the desk, luckily not broken. Sometimes the checking-out process could be very disagreeable, but this floor clerk was a friendly woman and she and Liza made little jokes about it.

"One bed," Liza said in Russian, "one bathtub . . ."

The woman laughed. She waved the porter toward the bags. "All in order. Thank you, Mademoiselle." She looked back at Uncle George's room. "The gentleman will return?"

"No," Liza said. "I'm meeting him downstairs." She gave the clerk both keys.

"Very well."

Liza gathered up her mac, her purse, Uncle George's camera, and her beret, and followed the porter. There was no room for her in the lift. It was a busy time, people going down to the dining room or out for the evening, and it was several minutes before she got the lift for herself. On the lower level she saw the two suitcases stacked near the door. The porter asked her what time she was going out.

"Bring me your car number when you get it from Intourist," he told her.

She went back upstairs to the main lobby to wait out

the time that was left. She tried to imagine what the Clown was doing. She could imagine all too well how he was feeling. She got up restlessly and walked the length of the big lobby. In the Intourist room she could see the young woman who had given her a bad time about the plane tickets. She either worked very long hours or on a very mixed-up schedule. It occurred to her that if the woman made her wait again when she went for the car number, the Clown would be left waiting outside the entrance, and that would not be good. But there was no sense worrying about that. From here on, there was nothing she could do except cope with each situation as it came up.

Just to be doing something, she looked through a big stack of postcards already stamped, and finally bought half a dozen, although she didn't want them. She'd give them to Walter; he collected stamps in a rather casual way. She went outside to check on the weather. Still that fine, misty summer rain. She hoped it would last. Poor Uncle George, getting wet. But by now he should be safely inside the Teatr Mimiki with his actor friend.

At ten minutes of eight she went into the Intourist office. In contrast to the crowds that gathered there during the day, there were only a few people now, most of them gathered around the theater ticket desk.

She had hoped there would be someone else at the travel desk, but the woman with the stormy blue eyes was still there, reading a paperback book.

At five minutes of eight Liza approached her. When the woman looked up, Liza said, "I'm here to get the car number for the airport. Liza Parke and George Asher."

The woman glanced at her watch. "You are too early. Sit down."

"I'd just as soon stand," Liza said.

The woman flashed her a look and said, "Oh, you are that one."

Liza tried a smile. She didn't want to antagonize this woman now. "Yes," she said.

The woman gave an exaggerated sigh of resignation and picked up the phone. She spoke rapidly, and certainly longer, Liza thought, than was necessary to confirm a car. And she laughed merrily as if she and the person on the phone had wonderful jokes. At last she hung up and wrote a number on a piece of paper. She handed the paper to Liza. "Car twenty-three." And with a gleam of amusement she said, "Go, go. You will be late."

"Thank you," Liza said evenly.

In the lobby she breathed a sigh of relief. *That* was over. The clock said one minute of eight. Trying not to look hurried, she sauntered out to the sidewalk just outside the main entrance. With dismay she saw that the Clown was not there. How terrible if he had changed his mind! Perhaps at the last minute the whole thing seemed too risky.

"Good evening." A man had stepped out of the dark doorway that led to the far end of the lobby. She couldn't see him clearly, and she was badly frightened. Then he came toward her, into the light, and she almost wept with relief. It was the Clown. But he didn't look like himself. With his shoulders built up by the epaulets on the coat, and the coat itself buckled tightly around his waist, he seemed to have changed shape. It wasn't

Uncle George's shape but it wasn't the Clown's either.

"You look like the Great Gatsby," she said, laughing. "It's wonderful." He had made up his face so that it looked fuller and older, and he had produced quite authentic-looking sideburns. The hair was lighter than his own, more like Uncle George's. The cap was at just the right angle, shadowing his eyes, and he wore his glasses, now fogged with rain. "Uncle George, you look marvelous."

He started to speak but instead he went into a most convincing coughing fit. She thrust the tube of Vicks into his hand. "Rub a little on your throat. It does wonders."

He did as she said, making a face at the pungent smell.

"We have to go down to the lower level." She led him toward the big doors. At the sight of the huge lighted lobby he hesitated. "Don't worry. Everything's going like a dream." She gave him the passport. "The customs declaration is tucked inside."

In the lights of the lobby she glanced quickly at him and marveled again at the expert makeup. He simply did not look like himself. With any luck, he could pass for Uncle George on the basis of the passport picture.

She waited impatiently for a free lift. At three minutes past eight they got one and a moment later stepped out into the much darker lower lobby. The Clown reeked of Vicks and every now and then he coughed.

"Poor Uncle George," she said. He winked at her. She knew what he was doing. He was trying to keep her from being nervous, just as she was trying to do for him. The feeling that they were in this together, with everything staked on the outcome, was both frightening and somehow pleasant. It made a close bond between them. We're like two of the Three Musketeers, she thought.

She gave her slip of paper to the porter, and he took their bags outside. There was a moment's wait before a black car pulled up at the curb. The porter spoke to the young driver and then went back into the hotel, nodding his thanks to Liza for the tip. She got into the back seat of the car and motioned the Clown to get in beside her. While the driver was still struggling with the lock to the trunk of the car, she leaned toward the Clown and said, "Give me the little booklet." She took off her beret.

He looked around first but it was quite dark and there was no one in sight except the driver behind them who was now thumping the trunk to get it to open. He took a small flat package from his inside pocket. It was neatly wrapped in newspaper and secured with a rubber band. She slipped it into the space between the lining and the felt material of the beret. It was a little bigger than she had remembered. She had to pull loose a few more stitches. Then she pinned the lining to the beret carefully, so the pin wouldn't show. The Clown didn't watch her. He seemed concerned about the driver's attempts to get the trunk open. Liza herself turned to look, wondering if it could be some kind of delaying tactic, but as she turned the trunk lid suddenly flew up and apparently hit the driver because she heard his exclamation of pain.

When at last he had the luggage stowed away, he got into the driver's seat and started off. Liza tried to get a look at him, but he kept his head down and the rearview mirror was tilted so she couldn't see his face. He seemed to be quite young. He never spoke to them or, as far as she could tell, even glanced in their direction. She didn't know whether to be reassured or alarmed.

She began to talk to the Clown. "You mustn't talk now, Uncle George," she said, as she had told him that other night in the taxi. "You save your voice. That Vicks will help, I think. It's a rotten shame that you caught such a cold."

The Clown made an appropriate hoarse sound.

"No, don't talk. I think the airport is quite far out, so you just relax. Intourist always gets us there in plenty of time."

They drove through miles and miles of apartment houses. It was hard to believe there could be a housing shortage in Moscow when one saw these acres of apartments.

"I've forgotten how long it takes to get to Copenhagen," she said. "It seems to me it's three or four hours." She tried to think of what else she could tell him safely. "I've got the key to your suitcase in my wallet if you want it. That's a tricky lock so I didn't lock it."

He nodded. He was looking at her, but after the effort at acting natural in the lobby, he looked pale and tired. Part of the pallor was probably makeup, she thought, to match Uncle George's cold. She mentioned the weather. "Keep your coat collar up so you won't get chilled." He turned it up. "Walter will meet us at the airport in Copenhagen. It will be good to get home, won't it? I hope Harriet has made some spoon bread." At his blank look, she said, "You midwesterners don't know what good spoon bread is. You probably don't even have it. Does Aunt May ever cook spoon bread?"

He shook his head and made a hoarse sound.

So much for spoon bread, Liza thought. What shall I talk about now? They seemed to have been driving forever, but she knew the airport was a long way out. The Clown was leaning a little toward the window, intently watching everything through the rain.

Suddenly the driver swerved toward the curb at an entrance to the Metro. He braked the car and jumped out, leaving the engine running. Liza and the Clown stared at each other in alarm. The driver ran up to a uniformed Metro attendant who stood out of the rain just inside the entrance. Quickly the Clown rolled down his window. The driver shouted to the older man, and then repeated whatever he said. The other man called back to him and pointed.

"What did he say?" Liza said. The palms of her hands felt wet. What could have gone wrong? she thought.

The Clown leaned back, relaxed, and laughed. He rolled up the window as the rain splashed in. "He is lost."

"Lost!" She thought of all Intourist people as perfectly efficient, almost automatons in carrying out their tasks.

"He say, 'Where is damned airport?' " He stopped laughing. "Do not notice."

After another series of gestures and pointing, the driver ran back and got into the car and drove off fast. He didn't explain nor even look back at his passengers. He turned on the radio to a station playing old-fashioned Beatles-type rock music. It was turned up loud, so Liza and the Clown could not have heard each other without difficulty.

The man was driving quite fast now, even for a Russian, taking corners so sharply that his passengers were constantly being thrown off balance. Liza looked at her watch. Perhaps he was afraid he wouldn't get them there on time. He must be new at his job, and he was frightened. She felt sorry for him.

They were jerked forward abruptly as the car came around a corner and almost hit a parked road repair truck, a huge thing that filled up half the road. The Clown put out his hand quickly to keep Liza from bumping her head against the back of the front seat. The driver backed up in a squeal of tires and pulled around the truck. He was hunched over the wheel, his shoulders tense. Liza thought: if the KGB doesn't get us, the bad drivers will.

It seemed like hours before the driver finally turned off, suddenly and with a sideways skid, at a big sign announcing the airport. The rock group on the radio was playing a wailing number with electric guitars and drums and a male singer whose lyrics seemed to consist mostly of *"niet, niet, niet!"* sung in a rising crescendo of anguish with deafening drum accompaniment. Liza giggled. The Clown looked at her and rolled his eyes.

The car careened around the big airport terminal toward a gate. The driver shut off the radio, throwing them into a startling silence. He rolled down his window and answered the questions of the guard, who peered into the car at Liza and the Clown. He seemed to be scolding the driver, who answered him in sulky monosyllables. Then he waved them on.

They drove up to an annex on the back of the terminal, and the driver stopped. He looked at them for the first time and jerked his head toward the waiting room. Then he went around to the back of the car to get the luggage.

A man in a suede jacket with the collar turned up waited in the doorway as they ran for the building. It was raining quite hard, and he obviously had no intention of getting wet. He stepped back and motioned them into the big, barren room. About fifteen people were in the room, scattered around in small groups. There was a little office off the waiting room that said INTOURIST.

"Americans, eh?" the man said in Engish. "You are going to New York?"

"Copenhagen," Liza said. She was sure he knew quite well where they were going.

"Ah, yes. May I have your passports please." He glanced toward the car, where the driver was trying unsuccessfully to get the trunk open, the rain pouring down on him. "The driver will bring your luggage. You will take it over there." He pointed to a check-in desk. "Your plane leaves at 21:20 hours. You will be taken to the plane. Meanwhile, please be seated." He looked again at the bent figure of the driver, but he made no move to help him with the luggage. He took their passports into his office.

"Let's sit down," Liza said. She went over to some uncomfortable metal chairs. The Clown sat down beside her. Most of the people were either reading or looking at a television set in the corner. No one paid any attention to them.

"One always has to wait a while," Liza said, so he wouldn't worry.

The driver was visible from where they sat. He was pounding the trunk lid with his fist and then he kicked it. It flew up. The Clown shook his head sympathetically. The Intourist man went to the door and looked out. He said something to the driver in a scolding voice and then went away again. The driver set the bags inside the door. His wet coat clung to him and his hair was plastered down on his forehead. He gave them a sheepish look and went out. The car drove off quickly.

"I guess we take them to the check-in place. I can do it if you like."

"No, no," he said. And she realized he was right. It would look odd if he let her carry the two bags. She had just been thinking of keeping him away from any scrutiny.

He picked up both bags, and she followed him to the counter. Two women in uniform leaned against the partition, one of them in her twenties, the other a very short, broad middle-aged woman. They were chatting, and for several minutes they paid no attention to Liza and the Clown.

Then the younger one looked at them and said, "Your tickets."

Liza had hers in her hand but the Clown took a moment to get his out of his mackintosh pocket. Liza was nervous, but she was also amused because he was fumbling carelessly the way Uncle George would do. She glanced at him and marveled at how different he looked from himself. It wasn't just the makeup; he had taken on Uncle George's personality somehow, a little impatient, a little rattled but in the kind of way that blames it on the rest of the world rather than himself. He had caught the essence of Uncle George, and she sensed that in spite of his fear he was concentrating on playing the part.

He got the ticket out of its case and put it on the counter. He also put down the customs declaration, but the clerk said, "Not yet," and gave it back to him. He cleared his throat as if to speak but instead he managed a small coughing fit. He turned away as he coughed. It was all done quite naturally.

The young clerk examined the tickets and tagged the two bags. She gave them the baggage checks, but kept the tickets. That made Liza nervous for a minute but then she remembered that they always did that and they gave out no boarding passes because they ushered their passengers aboard the plane in person.

The older woman, who had a wide expressionless face and who apparently did not speak English, slung the two suitcases up onto a table and motioned to them with a jerk of her head. Liza took the Clown's arm. He was still struggling with a subdued cough and was facing away from the clerks.

"Customs inspection," she said. She was pleased that her voice sounded normal and casual. Her stomach muscles were so tense they ached.

Indifferently, as Uncle George would do it, and with none of the smiling eagerness of the real Clown, he turned and moved along to the table. The woman gestured to them to open their suitcases. The Clown had a moment of trouble with the catch, but he slapped it impatiently with the palm of his hand and when he tried it again, it opened.

As Liza had hoped, the inspector went through her case first. She took out the Berlitz book, the guidebook, the copy of *Persuasion,* and the letter addressed to Mackie and pushed them toward the other woman. She said something that Liza didn't catch. Liza glanced at the Clown. His face gave no hint that he had understood what she said. Perhaps he hadn't. There were so many different accents in Moscow, and Russian was a second language for him. She must ask him to speak Georgian for her some time. Some time when it was safe.

While the young clerk carefully studied the three books, leafing through them and now and then stopping to read a whole page, the customs clerk went through the other things in the suitcase, carelessly pulling them out and dumping them in a heap on the counter. Liza flinched when she saw her green linen dress pushed along the counter as if it were an old rag. She wanted to protest, but this was no time for that. The woman, who seemed to enjoy her work, turned out the contents of the zippered toilet case, dumping toothpaste, toothbrush, soap and makeup on the dirty counter. Meanwhile the younger woman had ripped open the envelope of the letter to Mackie and was reading it laboriously, moving her lips. It gave Liza pleasure that the letter was long and rather boring.

The inspector left Liza to repack her suitcase, while she moved on to George Asher's luggage. The Clown stood in a relaxed position, leaning a little against the counter, his hands in his coat pockets. He smelled strongly of Vicks and every few minutes he cleared his throat or blew his nose or managed a slight cough. It wasn't unnecessarily conspicuous, but he made it quite clear that here was an American with a cold.

The inspector pulled Uncle George's clothes out, looked inside the Dopp-Kit, ignored the film. Then when she had made a thorough mess of everything, she walked away. The Clown glanced at Liza.

As the young clerk pushed the books and the letter toward her, Liza said, "Shall we pack up now?"

"Yes. Pack." The clerk waited, looking bored, while Liza finished and the Clown repacked and closed his suitcase. "Customs declaration," the clerk said.

Liza spread hers out on the counter. The Clown found his and did the same.

"Your purse." She dumped the contents of Liza's purse out on the counter. "You have rubles?"

"No, we exchanged the rubles that were left."

The clerk searched in every corner of the purse, opened the passport case and went through its pockets, counted Liza's Danish and American money and checked it against the declaration. She even went through the small change purse.

Liza hadn't thought about the Clown's wallet. Whatever he had, she hoped it wouldn't look Russian. She stole a glance when he put it down. It was a plain brown leather wallet that could have been bought in any country.

The clerk counted his American money, searched the pockets of his mackintosh, leaning across the counter to thrust her hands in his pockets. For a second he looked quite startled, but even Uncle George would have looked startled at that. She told the Clown to hold the coat open, while she checked the big inside pocket. There were no pockets in his pullover. Liza was nervous about whether she would check his trouser pockets. They were Russian trousers and, at least to Liza, they looked it. But the woman only looked, apparently satisfying herself that there were no suspicious bulges that might be rubles. She made him take the camera off his shoulder, but it was only the inside of the case, not the camera itself, that interested her. She gave it back to him, satisfied at last.

"Sit down now. You will be called." She swung the suitcases off the counter and left them beside the weighing scale. In a few minutes a man came in and took them away.

The Clown followed Liza back to their chairs. Liza offered him an English-language newspaper that she had picked up. He turned up his coat collar, slumped a little in his chair, and read the paper. She wondered if he could really read English, or if he found the Roman alphabet as difficult as she found the Cyrillic.

She looked around the big, ugly room. Some Germans were talking, in a little group, nearby. She couldn't tell what the other passengers were, but most of them didn't look to her like Americans. There was one man in his twenties, sprawled in his chair, reading a paperback copy of *The Odessa File*. He looked like an American because of his clothes. Another man in a tight-fitting dark topcoat, tight trousers, and a black derby hat, looked like a Middle-European spy in an old Hollywood movie. He was with a quite beautiful older woman. They walked past Liza, he twirling a folded umbrella. For a minute she couldn't place the language they were speaking, but then she realized it was Hungarian. He looked at her with the kind of sly smile that Hungarians often had, as if they harbored some very important secret that would change the world. Liza smiled. She liked Hungarians. They had flair. And, she remembered with a pang, Budapest had wonderful food. She was very hungry and very sick of Russian food. But Copenhagen had wonderful food, too, and

Harriet was a skillful cook. Oh, it would be good to be home again!

Two priests came in with their suitcases. The Intourist man stopped them, took their passports, and directed them to the check-in counter. Liza watched them in idle curiosity. It surprised her that the authorities would let priests in, they worried so much about their people being polluted by religious ideas. These were plump, middle-aged, pleasant-faced men, who looked the way she thought of priests as looking. "Benevolent" was the word she was trying to think of. They were, she guessed, either Irish or American. She watched them as they tried to make small talk and little jokes with the two Russian women. It was all lost. The older one didn't understand them, and wouldn't have given up her scowl for anything; and the younger one was bored. After a while they gave up and addressed their remarks to each other. Their good humor was like a little patch of sunshine in that dreary room. She saw that the Clown also was watching them.

When the customs people finally finished with them, the priests walked past Liza and the Clown to some chairs that were empty. They both smiled and nodded, and the younger one said, "Good evening."

"Good evening," Liza said.

The Clown nodded.

They seemed like nice men, but she hoped they wouldn't want to strike up a conversation. It would be awkward to have to explain the Clown's inability to talk. And her state of mind was such that she was not ready to accept a friendly priest as a friendly priest. In this world things were not what they seemed. But the men stayed by themselves until at last a small, thin woman appeared from somewhere and imperiously beckoned to the priests, to Liza and the Clown, and to the man who was reading *The Odessa File*.

Liza looked at the baggage clerk, who caught her look.

"Go with her," the clerk said. "Go." She made a motion as if to hurry them. The thin woman was already disappearing out the door.

"My word," said the younger priest as they caught up with Liza and the Clown, "she is in a hurry."

Liza smiled and nodded. The woman had jumped into an airport bus and was waiting for them impatiently.

The older priest said to the Clown, "Are you folks Americans?" He had a slight Irish brogue.

Before the Clown had to answer, Liza said, "Yes, we are. My uncle has laryngitis . . ." She touched her throat to be sure the Clown knew what she had said. "He caught a bad cold. He can't talk without croaking." She laughed, and hoped she hadn't overdone it. She wished the priests would move ahead, but they walked along beside her and when they got into the bus, they sat beside her.

"We are from Boston," the younger one said. He was looking at the Clown.

"Oh, yes," Liza said. She was trying desperately not to break into chatter. "We're from Virginia. At least I am. My uncle lives in Wisconsin." The younger priest's scrutiny alarmed her.

"I would have thought you were English," he said.

"I went to school in England."

"Oh, I see." The bus started with a lurch. The priest fell against her and apologized.

"That's all right." She straightened her beret, frightened at how near it had come to falling off. She touched the hard place in the top that the Clown's little red passport made. Perhaps he had been right, and she shouldn't have risked bringing it. She was worried too about their passports, which had not been given back to them. She tried to remember whether the Intourist people had kept them until after they were aboard the plane last year. But she hadn't noticed.

The bus came to a stop alongside a big Aeroflot jet. The thin woman, unsmiling, waved them off. At the steps to the plane, Liza, who was first, started to go up. The Clown was behind her. The woman, in a flow of angry Russian, grabbed her arm and stopped her.

As Liza turned to see what the matter was, her heart almost stopped. Four men in Red Army uniforms and carrying rifles were running toward the plane. She didn't dare look at the Clown.

"What now, for goodness' sake?" the older priest said. "We'll never get out of this country."

The soldiers pushed past them and ran up the steps and into the plane. From where she stood, Liza could see one of them poking his gun under the seats, and looking in the rack above. Then he disappeared.

"They're looking for bombs," the older priest said. He giggled nervously.

"Or spies in the luggage rack," the younger one said.

Liza wished desperately that they would be quiet. She thought the soldiers would never get off the plane. She was terribly frightened. She could feel the Clown standing close behind her, and although he stood quite still, she could feel his fear. It seemed to her that everybody must be able to tell how afraid they were.

Then the soldiers came down the steps. The last one, older than the others, looked sharply at Liza. Then he looked at the Clown, and for a moment he hesitated. He asked a question in Russian. He did it so unexpectedly that Liza was terrified that the Clown would automatically answer. She thought the soldier said, "What place are you going to?"

But instantly the younger priest stepped toward the soldier. He said, "We are Americans, sir. We do not understand your language. May we please board the plane now? One of our number has a severe cold. He should not be standing in this rain."

The soldier stared at him, muttered something, and moved on. The priest said to the Intourist woman, "We may board now, I presume," and he started up the steps.

The Intourist woman pushed in front of him and scampered up. She turned then and motioned the passengers on impatiently, as if it had been they who caused the delay. The priest chuckled. "Wonderful," he said.

The stewardess at the top of the steps ushered them to seats. The plane was already nearly full of passengers, many of them in some kind of uniform, not an official uniform, Liza thought, but perhaps some club or something. The priest looked back at her.

"A Russian band, I believe," he said. "I saw the instruments being loaded."

"Oh," she said. There would not, of course, be many Americans on the Copenhagen plane. She hadn't really thought about who the other passengers might be.

The Clown was behind her, but she made room for him to go into the seats first so he could sit by the window. He would be less noticeable there, and people wouldn't be likely to talk to him. The two priests took seats across the aisle.

Almost at once the plane swung around and taxied toward the runway. The stewardess gave her "welcome aboard" and safety instruction speech first in Russian, then in Danish, and then in English. Behind Liza an elderly couple were talking quietly in Danish. It reassured Liza to hear the language again.

The Clown took off Uncle George's cap and put it in the seat beside him. Liza glanced quickly at his hair. He caught her look and put the cap back on again. He did look all right without it, but no sense taking chances. His glasses were so fogged with rain, he had to clean them but she noticed he didn't get them entirely clean. Surely they would get their passports back soon. She longed to ask the priest if he had his, but she thought she had better not. They were genuine priests she felt sure. That Boston accent with the trace of Irish would be hard to fake. But it was better not to speak, not to call attention to herself. She was grateful to the priest for getting rid of the soldier.

"Here we go," she said to the Clown, as the plane started down the runway.

He gave her a wan smile, looking pale and strained. Most of the time he sat hunched forward with his face close to the window, looking out at the rain-blurred lights. She reminded him to fasten his seat belt.

The heavy plane seemed to pull itself up into the air with a shudder. Liza ate the piece of candy the

133

stewardess had handed out. Russian candy was awfully good; she wished she had taken two. The Clown still had his in his hand, as if he had forgotten it was there. He leaned forward still more, as the plane climbed, looking down at the lights of Russia. When the plane came through the clouds into a clear, starry sky, he leaned back in his seat and closed his eyes.

After about half an hour the stewardess brought their passports and the Copenhagen-New York portion of Uncle George's plane ticket. Liza took them with a show of indifference, but her heart leaped with relief She noticed that the priests got theirs back at the same time, so it must have been just routine. She began to relax a little. But they were still in Russia, and they would remain technically in Russia until they got off the plane. She didn't dare think yet "we've made it." Uncle George could still come home early for some reason and raise a ruckus and Intourist would realize that some impostor was on this plane with George Asher's ticket and passport. They were not in the clear yet.

Both priests had gone to sleep. Liza wished she could sleep, too, but she was tense. Although the Clown kept his eyes closed, she knew he was awake. It was very hard for him to be leaving his country. For the first time she began to think about the Clown in Denmark. Perhaps the circus in Copenhagen would hire him. Or even better, the circus in Zurich, if there was one. She had never come across it, but at the school they lived rather a life apart. If he were in Zurich, she could see him more often; but if he were in Copenhagen, she would see him during vacations at least. Perhaps she could persuade him to live at her apartment. Harriet and Walter would love him.

When they had been aloft about an hour, the stewardesses brought dinner. Liza touched the Clown on the arm so he would be ready for it. He started and opened his eyes wide as if for a moment he didn't know where he was.

"Dinner," she said. She put down his tray for him.

The meal was simple but good—cold chicken, potatoes, salad, bread and butter, a glass of white wine, tea, and some kind of Russian pudding. Liza was hungry. She ate it all. The Clown ate his, too, except for the pudding, which he offered to her. He looked a little better after he had eaten.

"Good meal," she said to him. He nodded. "Cold chicken was just the right thing. Are you feeling any better?"

He smiled and nodded again.

"Don't try to talk. Rest your throat." She said that as the stewardess leaned past her to pick up the Clown's tray.

The younger priest beamed at her. "You folks going straight on to New York?"

"No," Liza said. "We're stopping in Copenhagen."

"Beautiful city. We're going on to London, and then to Boston on Saturday."

"I hope you'll enjoy London," Liza said politely.

"Oh, yes. Always enjoy London. It's a marvelous city." He had bright, shrewd eyes that seemed to see right into her. "Where do you go to school?"

"In Zurich now, but after next year I'll be at the University of Virginia."

"Oh, yes. Fine, fine. Splendid school. Lovely country, Virginia."

"Yes." Although she believed he was a Boston priest, she wished she could end the conversation. He asked so many questions.

In a couple of minutes the other priest ended the conversation for her. "Stop your chatter, Father," he said good-humoredly. "People are trying to sleep."

"Oh!" The younger priest raised his eyebrows and put his finger to his lips. "*Shh!*"

Liza laughed. He was really a sweet little man. He folded his hands over his plump stomach and obediently closed his eyes, but not before he had given her a solemn wink.

Liza closed her eyes too, slumping down in the seat and trying to stretch out her long legs in a comfortable position. She was never happy on a plane because of the limited leg room. She was sure she wouldn't sleep, but she did wake after a while to find her head on the Clown's shoulder. Embarrassed she jerked upright, but the Clown gave no sign of noticing. He had his eyes closed still and his head turned toward the window. She looked at her watch. They must be out of Russia by now.

She slept again, and this time the stewardess's voice on the loud speaker woke her. She was announcing the descent into Copenhagen. People began to stir. The Clown opened his eyes and looked at her.

"We're almost there," she said in a low voice.

He looked as if he couldn't believe it. She could hardly believe it herself. Had it really worked? They just had to get off the plane now, go into Danish customs, and they would be safe. She thought of Walter, probably at the airport already waiting for her. How surprised he would be to see the Clown instead of Uncle George. She hoped Walter wouldn't disapprove. She set great store by his approval.

The plane banked sharply and then began a steep descent to the lighted field. It was not raining here. The sky was clear. She held the arms of the seat to steady herself. Aeroflot always seemed to go straight down or straight up for landing and takeoff. There was a bump as the plane hit the runway. Thump, thump. In three languages they were requested to remain in their seats until the plane stopped, to keep their seat belts fastened, to refrain from smoking until they were in the terminal.

Liza buttoned her mackintosh and touched the beret for luck. The Clown also buttoned his coat and sat up straight. He had a strange look on his face, which she couldn't quite read, a mixture of elation and sorrow and certainly still some fear probably. She would ask Walter what the Clown should do to make his arrival official and to ask for sanctuary. It must be the Danish police he should go to. Perhaps he could do it in the morning. He looked so tired.

People were getting up and collecting their things. Liza waited until most of them had moved past her before she got up. The younger priest, already in the aisle, smiled back at her. "God bless," he said.

"Thank you," she said.

"You'll be fine now." He nodded reassuringly, and she wondered what he thought about them. She was quite sure he knew something was not quite as it ought to be. Well, she would never know.

The Clown bent his head to get out from under the

low rack. He glanced around him quickly, noticing all the Russian faces of the members of the band, some of them cheerful and excited about their trip, some of them phlegmatic. She wondered if it took a Russian to know a Russian. Just in case of that danger, she lingered, fussing with her coat, until they had all filed past her.

"I'm going to stop in the terminal and send a cable to my friend at the embassy in Moscow," she said to the Clown. "So she'll know we've arrived." When he looked puzzled, she added, "She'll tell. . . ." She shook her head and smiled. "It's all right. I'll tell you later." She was going to wire Meredith that she would leave Uncle George's passport, ticket to New York, and suitcase at the airline passenger desk. She would also wire Aunt May that Uncle George was all right but had been delayed.

She was sorry she'd started to tell the Clown that. Of course he didn't understand, and she couldn't explain here. He still looked worried, so she said again, "It's all right. It's about the friend in Moscow." Now he got it, and his face cleared. He nodded two or three times.

They went down the long passageway that connected the plane to the airport and followed the crowd into customs. There was a short wait for the luggage. After it came, they queued up at the booth to get their passports stamped. This was a tense moment, although Liza didn't think they would send the Clown back even if they noticed the passport. But nothing occurred. The clerk glanced at them both and stamped their passports. They went into the big room where the customs inspectors were. They were almost the last ones, and to Liza's relief, the man waved them on through without an examination of their luggage.

Liza felt so elated and relieved, she wanted to shout. Instead she grabbed the Clown's wrist and squeezed it. "We did it!" she said.

"Can I speak?"

"Yes! Speak, shout, do a cartwheel! No, I guess not just yet." She was laughing with joy. And then she saw Walter coming toward her. She ran to him and threw her arms around him.

Walter held her off, laughing. "What is this? You've only been gone a week." Then he saw the Clown and the laughter in his face changed to amazement.

"Walter, this a friend of mine who's going to stay with us . . ."

"Where's Mr. Asher?"

"Walter, it's a terribly long story, and I can't tell you now."

Shaking his head Walter held out his hand. "Well, hello anyway." He smiled. "You took me by surprise. You looked a little like Mr. Asher . . . I thought . . ." He broke off, puzzled.

"Don't think now, Walter." Liza patted his arm. "Everything's fine. Where's the car?"

Walter grinned. "In the NO PARKING zone in front of the main entrance."

"You two go out to the car, and I'll be there in just a sec. I've got to send a cable to Aunt May, and leave Uncle George's suitcase . . ." She glanced at the Clown. He looked white and shaky, almost as if he would faint.

"Where is your aunt?" Walter said.

"In Wisconsin." She turned Walter around to face the door. "Will you take my suitcase?" And to the Clown she said, "Everything's fine. Walter will look after you. I'll be there in a minute." She picked up

Uncle George's suitcase. "Oh, the passport," she said to the Clown. "And the plane ticket."

He gave them to her. His hand was shaking.

"Fine. Thank you. Now you go with Walter." She saw him look around the airport, as if he were still expecting to be arrested. "You're in Denmark. Everything's fine." She left them and found the airline reservations counter she needed. In what her father used to call "the bottom-less pit of a woman's purse" she found an envelope big enough for the passport and ticket. She put a rubber band around the envelope and wrote Uncle George's name and home address on it.

It took a minute to persuade the clerk to hold the things until the next day, but she convinced him finally that it was an emergency and that her uncle wouldn't know where to find them if she put them in a locker. "He's in Russia at the moment," she told him. "It's hard to get hold of him. Things got a bit mixed up."

He took her phone number in case Uncle George failed to show up.

She went next to the counter where she could send cables. She sent one to Aunt May saying, "If Uncle George is a little delayed, don't worry. Everything under control. Love, *Liza*." The other one went to Meredith, saying, "Sorry about mixup. George Asher's passport ticket luggage at Copenhagen SAS reservations desk. *Liza Parke*." Not that that will enlighten them any, she thought, but it should straighten out his problems somewhat. She hurried toward the main entrance. The poor Clown, poor darling, he'd looked as if he were in a state of shock. She stopped and took off her beret, stepped out of the main aisle and took the pin out of the lining. She had to know his name. It took her a moment to translate the Cyrillic. Grigol Vakhtang. She said it softly aloud. Grigol Vakhtang.

Walter and the Clown were in the car when she ran out to join them. She climbed into the back seat of the little Austin Mini when the Clown got out to let her in. She was feeling excited and happy now, almost giddy with release from strain. "Hurry home, Walter," she said. "I've got a long story to tell you."

"I don't doubt that, Liza," Walter said. He grinned at the Clown. "She's always up to something."

Liza leaned her arms on the back of the Clown's seat as Walter expertly wheeled the Mini in a wide circle and got onto the road. "Walter, there's one thing. If a person is defecting from Russia, who does he go to? And does he have to go to them immediately or can it wait for morning?"

Walter gave a low whistle and it was a minute before he answered. "Liza, you really *have* been up to something."

"Does he go to the Danish police?"

"I think so. We'd better drop in and have a little chat with them before we go home."

"It couldn't wait? He's awfully tired."

"Better be safe, honey." He looked at the Clown. "I think it would be better if you register with the police right away."

The Clown looked back at Liza, puzzled.

She laughed. "Walter, nobody understands that outrageous Virginia accent. I've been telling you for years." And to the Clown she said, "Walter thinks you'd better check in with the police tonight." He looked alarmed.

141

"It's all right. Just routine. But then you'll be all legal."
She smiled at him reassuringly. She'd be glad when he
got that makeup off and looked like himself again. "The
Danish police are nice. I'll go in with you."

He nodded and smiled, but she could tell it was an
effort. As the car sped through the outskirts of the city,
she said, "Walter drives like a Dane. Very fast but
very good."

The Clown said, "In Russia, also very fast but not
always so good."

"I know. Sometimes terrible. I think some nationali-
ties are good with cars and others aren't."

"The ones that are good," Walter said dryly, "are apt
to be the ones that have 'em."

The lights of the long, tree-lined avenue glowed
softly in the gray night. "How's Harriet?" Liza asked.

"Fine. She would have come, but she had something
in the oven."

"Spoon bread," Liza said.

"Well, no, I don't think so. Why spoon bread?"

"Oh, it popped into my mind back in Moscow when
I was trying to talk and sound normal. I chattered away
about spoon bread."

"I don't understand what your Aunt May and Uncle
George are doing in Wisconsin."

"Just Aunt May."

"Oh? Where's Uncle George?"

"Walter, it will take a long time to tell you. As soon
as we get home, all right?"

"All right." He drove more slowly for a while. "Somewhere along here I've seen a police station. . . . Ah,
there it is." He made a right turn and drove into the

circular tarmac in front of the station. "You want me to come in or not?"

"No, you don't need to. And Walter, don't worry."

"Okay. I don't suppose you'd do anything too illegal." He raised his eyebrows. "What am I saying?"

She laughed and climbed out of the car. "Just a touch." She gave the Clown his Soviet identification card. He was looking suspiciously at the entrance to the police station. "It's all right, honestly."

She went ahead of him into the building and found a police officer sitting at a desk. She took a deep breath. "This is my friend Grigol Vakhtang from the Soviet Union. He wants to defect to Denmark."

12

The Danish police officer blinked. "Mademoiselle?"

"Do you speak English?" Liza asked him.

"Slowly."

She repeated slowly what she had said. His eyes widened.

"One moment." He got up and went into another room.

"We might as well sit down," Liza said to the Clown.

"What shall I tell them?" He stood looking down at her, frowning a little.

"The whole story," Liza said. "The truth. They will be sympathetic."

He nodded, but he didn't look entirely convinced. "They will not send me back?"

"No. They would not do that. Don't worry."

The officer came back and beckoned to them. "Will you please come in this room?" When they had followed him into a large office, he closed the door. Another man sat behind a massive desk. He rose, shook hands with them both, and gave them his name.

"Does the Russian gentleman speak English?" he asked Liza.

"Yes. French also." Her heart was beating fast. She was sure what she had told the Clown was true, that they would be sympathetic, but she was nervous nevertheless.

"Your name, sir?" he asked the Clown.

The Clown spelled it for him and answered the questions about age, address, occupation. He showed his Soviet passport.

When the Clown said that he was a circus clown, the police officer looked up and smiled. "Very nice."

The Clown began to relax a little under the other man's courtesy. He told him, when he was asked, that he was to have been arrested by the KGB because he had applied for an exit visa. He told him about his friend's being questioned and about eluding the KGB man. His voice grew stronger as he talked and he seemed now quite calm. He explained about the help Liza had given him.

When the Clown had finished, the officer looked at Liza. "Your name and address, Mademoiselle? Age? You go to school?" He examined her passport. She answered his questions.

"The story this man has told me, this Mr. Vakhtang, you agree?"

"Yes."

"The man, your uncle . . . his name?" He wrote it down. "And where is he now?"

"In Moscow, I'm afraid. I ditched him."

"Ah. Poor Mr. Asher!"

"I know. I'm awfully sorry. But it was the only way I could think of to save Mr. Vakhtang."

"And why did you wish to save Mr. Vakhtang?"

She swallowed. It was a question she hadn't anticipated. "Well . . ." she said. He waited. "He's such a lovely clown."

The police officer smiled. She didn't dare look at the Clown.

"Have you notified anyone about Mr. Asher?"

She explained what she had done, and he nodded. For some time he wrote on the pad of paper in front of him. Then he said, "Mr. Vakhtang, I will read you what I have written here. Then you may read it for yourself. Then if you will, please, I would like you to sign it." He read, slowly, the account of the story the Clown had given him and the information Liza had added. "Do I have it right?"

"Yes," the Clown said. "I cannot read English. If the young lady would read it for me? . . ." He looked at Liza.

She read it carefully. "Yes, just what he said."

The Clown signed his name and filled in the date. Then Liza also signed it.

The officer pushed back his chair and rose. "We will call you. He will be with you, Mademoiselle?"

"Yes."

"You will write your telephone number, please." He

held out his hand to the Clown. "Welcome to Denmark, Mr. Vakhtang."

Anxiously the Clown said, "It will be all right?"

"There will be formalities, but you have no need to worry. Denmark is hospitable." He shook hands with Liza. "You are a very brave young lady. Mr. Vakhtang was fortunate that you went to the circus."

"Yes," the Clown said, looking at Liza with emotion. "Without her. . . ." He shook his head.

The officer walked to the door with them, his hand on the Clown's shoulder. "I hope you will like our country."

"I am very grateful. . . ." The Clown's eyes filled with tears. He took off his rain-streaked glasses and wiped his eyes. "I am sorry."

"Not at all, my dear fellow, not at all."

When they got back to the car, the Clown got into the back seat and sat slumped down, his long legs pulled up. "It is hard to believe," he said. "Such kindness."

"The Danes are lovely people," Liza said. It hurt her to see tears in his eyes. "You'll like them. They laugh a lot, and they're very charming. Aren't they, Walter."

"Oh, they're great. How did it go?"

"Beautifully." Liza clasped her hands together. "I can't wait to get home. I wonder what Harriet is cooking."

"I don't know, but the flat smelled like Virginia," Walter said. He gunned the engine, and the little car sped up the avenue.

"The very first thing," Liza said, "is that the Clown— Mr. Vakhtang, I mean—gets to take off his makeup.

And give him some of Dad's Courvoisier, Walter. And then Harriet's lovely food."

"Makeup?" Walter said.

"Yes. His Uncle George makeup. He's really much younger."

"I feel," Walter said, "as if I'd walked into the last reel of the late-late show."

"You'll get the rehash shortly. I can't tell it all to you and then again to Harriet." She had begun to feel very tired. It seemed like a week since she'd gone to bed.

Her eyes had begun to close before Walter turned into the parking area behind their flat. Then she woke up with a jerk. "We're here." She leaned forward and looked up to the flat on the top floor, which was lighted. "Harriet's waiting for us."

The Clown had been silent since they left the police station, but now he roused himself. "You must be tired, Liza."

Liza looked at him with her eyes shining. It was the first time he had used her name. Until tonight he hadn't known it, just as she hadn't known his. It seemed like the marking of a new phase in their friendship.

Harriet was waiting at the door. The living room, behind her, had never looked more attractive to Liza. And Harriet in a new soft apricot-colored robe, looked prettier than ever. Liza hugged her and introduced her to the Clown. Harriet concealed her reactions more expertly than Walter had done; she didn't even look surprised.

"Come in, come in, everybody," she said. "Food's sitting on the stove. You've been forever. Was the plane late?" She had a soft Virginia voice.

The Clown glanced around the living room and Liza saw with pleasure that he liked it.

"No, plane wasn't late," Walter said. "Liza had to attend to a little international espionage. She's taken up smuggling."

"Oh, good," Harriet said. "This household was getting dull. What we need is a little intrigue. Walter, why don't you take Liza's guest and his . . ." She noticed that he had no bag, but she slid over it easily. "I think John's room is in pretty good shape. I cleaned in there last week."

It gave Liza a strange feeling that the Clown should be moving into her father's room. But of course there were only the three bedrooms.

The Clown thanked Harriet and followed Walter up to the second level of the flat, where the bedrooms were.

"That man looks mighty tired," Harriet said. "How are you, darlin'?"

"Fine," Liza said. "What have you been cooking? It smells like hushpuppies."

"Among other things. Come on out in the kitchen and talk to me."

By the time they had put the food on the table Walter came downstairs to say that the Clown was going to take a shower and go straight to bed. Liza was disappointed. She had wanted him to enjoy Harriet's delicious meal.

"Let him be, Liza," Walter said. "He looks real beat."

"Walter can take him up a tray," Harriet said, "in case he gets to hankering after a bite to eat later on."

When they started to eat, Walter looked at Liza expectantly, but she wanted to wait and tell her story after the meal. Then she waited until Walter had taken a tray upstairs.

He came down shaking his head. "Thought I'd got in the wrong compartment," he said. "That fellow sure looks different without his Uncle George."

Liza laughed. "I told you."

They went into the living room and Liza curled up on the big comfortable divan that she and her father had picked out for this flat.

Walter stood with his back to the fireplace. "And now," he said, "as the house lights dim and the great crimson curtain slowly rises, the audience waits in nail-biting expectancy, while the stage lights reveal that spell-binding teller of tales of high adventure—MISS LIZA PARKE!"

Liza giggled and Harriet said, "Hush, Walter. Let the child talk."

Liza told them the whole story, every detail that she could remember. They listened without any interruption. When she was finished, Walter said softly, "Well, bless my soul." Then after a moment he added, "The trouble you could have got into."

Liza was waiting for Harriet's comment. For several minutes Harriet was silent, looking down at her folded hands, her face expressionless. Then she looked up and said, "You did fine. Your father would be pleased."

Later Liza knelt by the open window of her bedroom waiting for the beautiful Copenhagen bells to strike the hour. The air felt fresh on her face. Below her in the narrow cobbled street four young men with arms around each other made their unsteady way, singing a drinking song. Now and then a late taxi dashed down the cobbled street. Otherwise it was quiet.

She rested her head on her arms and almost fell asleep, but then the bells began to chime. She had listened to bells in many places but none moved her as much as these. She counted the long, slow, silvery strokes. She hoped the Clown heard them and felt cheered.

She looked out over the rooftops, dark against the gray sky. The short night was nearly gone. "Be good to him, Copenhagen," she said softly. She got into bed and fell instantly asleep.

13

Liza slept late. When she got downstairs, the Clown had finished breakfast and was answering Harriet's questions about Georgian cooking. He jumped up when Liza came in.

"Good morning, Liza."

"Good morning . . ." She hesitated. ". . . Grigol." She felt shy, using his name. "Did you sleep well?"

"Oh, yes. Such a beautiful room."

She was relieved that he looked like himself again. Walter or Harriet had gotten him one of her father's short-sleeved sports shirts, which fitted quite well. She had given away most of her father's clothes because Harriet said she should, but had kept some sweaters and jackets and shirts that she had particularly liked.

"I'm getting a crash course in Georgian cooking," Harriet said. "How does a nice bowl of *khartcho* grab you? Followed by *tabaka,* which in case you don't know, is chicken that you cook between two firebricks."

The Clown laughed. "Already you are expert. But no firebricks here, is it so?"

Harriet smiled. "It is so. No firebricks."

Liza could tell that Harriet liked the Clown.

"But your cooking," the Clown said, "it is superb. No need to learn more."

After breakfast Liza told the Clown she would like to take him to Tivoli Gardens. She explained as well as she could what the Gardens were like. "But you really have to see them. There's so much, I can't describe it all."

The Clown's look of uneasiness returned. He glanced toward the window. "You think it is all right to go out? No danger?"

"I'm sure it's all right. And you don't want to stay cooped up inside on a lovely day like this." She felt it was important to get him out, something like getting back on a horse after you've been thrown.

After the first few minutes outside the Clown seemed to relax. He was charmed by the narrow, medieval-looking streets, the fountains in the big square on Hans Christian Andersen Boulevard, the many bicyclists who sped around the city with almost as much verve and daring as the motorists. He told Liza about the beautiful fountains in Tbilisi.

"In Georgia we are in high mountains," he said. "Tbilisi is all around framed by mountains, and there are fountains and waterfalls everywhere." He sat down, looking up at the big stone dragon from whose mouth came a stream of sparkling water. "There are oranges and lemons growing, and many, many flowers everywhere. In the old days the great Russian writers came to Georgia for the weather. Very warm and nice."

In the flower market he started to buy Liza a bouquet and then remembered he had no money. His face fell. "It is bad, that I could not bring money."

"Why don't you change that U.S. money I gave you into Danish," Liza said. "You can pay me back when you're working again." She took him to one of the banks that change money. Since he had no passport, she changed it herself and gave it to him when they were outside. "There. Now you are a Dane with money in your pocket."

"No," he said, "I am a Georgian." But he cheered up when he returned to the flower market to buy her an armful of flowers.

Like all tourists, he was overwhelmed by the charm and diversity of Tivoli Gardens. Although there were many people about, the big park absorbed them easily. They found an open-air acrobatic show, which the Clown watched with great pleasure.

"They are very good," he said.

"Some evening we'll come see the pantomime theater," Liza said. She led him around a pretty pond to an outdoor restaurant at noon, where they had smørrebrød and Danish coffee. The Clown liked the open sandwich so much, Liza got him a second one, with anchovies, cucumbers, and sliced tomatoes. Near them a band played lively music.

After lunch they rented a little boat, and the Clown

154

rowed Liza around the pond. Other people were out in boats, relaxed and friendly in the warm sunshine. The lines of strain in the Clown's face began to ease away.

He was amused when Liza showed him the Fun House, where for a small fee customers could relieve their frustrations by smashing china.

"I've tried it," Liza said. "It's better than a psychiatrist."

It was four o'clock when they strolled back to the flat. As they came up the walk, they noticed two men apparently waiting for someone. One of them had a camera. The Clown stopped short.

"Who are those men?" he said in a low voice.

"I don't know." They looked like press, but she wasn't sure. She watched them uneasily as they came toward her.

The man without the camera said in American English, "Are you Liza Parke?"

"Yes."

"And that is Vakhtang, I suppose?" He smiled broadly at the Clown. "Mr. Vakhtang?"

The Clown didn't answer. He waited stiffly, frowning.

"Who are you?" Liza said. Over their shoulders she saw Walter come out the front door.

"I'm with a wire service." The man flipped open his leather case and showed her his identification. He showed it also to the Clown, but the Clown didn't look at it.

"He's from the newspapers," Liza said to the Clown.

The Clown stepped back. "No. Nothing to say."

"What is it you want?" Liza said.

"A story." The man was quite pleasant, but he was obviously not going to be easy to discourage. "I heard about your fantastic trick, getting Vakhtang out of Russia."

"It was hardly a trick," Liza said sharply.

The photographer took a picture of them. The Clown threw up his arm to hide his face.

"Liza," Walter said, coming up behind the men. "Let me talk to you a minute."

"Oh, it's you, Mr. Jackson," the newspaperman said. "Will you tell the young lady and Mr. Vakhtang that we don't mean any harm?"

Walter took Liza by the arm and beckoned to the Clown. They went around the corner of the building to a small rose garden. "They've been here all afternoon," Walter said. "I tried to get rid of them, but no way."

"How did they know about us?"

"Somebody at the police station, maybe. I don't know. They always find out. And it looks to them like a great human interest story." Walter made a face.

"Tell them to go away," the Clown said.

"I can tell them but they won't go. I know how you feel, but I'll tell you what I honestly think. It's better to give them the story you want them to have than to leave them to piece together their own. Your father used to say, Liza, don't antagonize the press if it isn't necessary."

Liza was trying to think. "I suppose they want to interview us."

"Yes. And if you do it, don't tell them anything that isn't true. You can leave things out but don't invent. They're not stupid." To the Clown he said, "I recommend talking to them, and I'll tell you why. It's an international wire service, and the story will hit papers in England and the States as well as here. I see it as a kind of protection for you."

"Protection?" The Clown was still frowning. He kept glancing back.

"Yes. If the KGB has any ideas about getting unpleasant with you, I think this would spoil their plans."

"I don't understand. They could then find me so easily."

"Well, they can find you anyway. You're a sitting duck. But if you become news, a lot of people would know if something happened to you. And I don't think the Russians like that kind of bad publicity. I think you're safer, Grigol, if you get a good press."

"He means," Liza explained, "the KGB aren't likely to go after you if they know it would be in all the papers if anything happened to you." She nodded slowly. "There's one other thing: every circus manager in the world, practically, will know that one of those wonderful Russian-trained clowns is temporarily unemployed. You'll get offers."

The Clown sat down on a white wrought-iron bench and leaned his head on his hands. "I must think."

They waited patiently. The more Liza considered what Walter had said, the more she thought he was right. And if the Clown got an offer from the Copenhagen Circus, or any of the circuses in Western Europe, how nice it would be. He would be happy and working, and she would be able to see him often.

The Clown looked up at her. "You would talk with them? I am not always sure of English."

"We can do it together," she said. "I'll fill in whenever you give me the signal."

He still looked doubtful. "We would not betray any of my friends?"

"Oh, of course not."

He sighed and stood up. "I do not trust press to tell truth, but I see it cannot be helped."

"I think our press is more likely to tell it the way you give it to them than perhaps yours is," Walter said, "although goodness knows, they don't have what you'd call a perfect track record."

They walked back to the front of the house, where the two men were sitting on the front steps. They jumped up as Liza and the Clown approached.

"Are we all set?" the reporter asked.

"Why don't you come up to the flat?" Liza said. "We can talk better there."

"Sure thing. That will be dandy."

They all went up together in the lift except the photographer with his equipment, who walked up the three flights of stairs. Harriet, waiting for them all in the doorway, gave the Clown an encouraging smile.

"They can't be all bad," Harriet said. "The photographer's from Atlanta."

Liza picked it up, trying to put the Clown at ease. "The man with the camera," she said, nodding toward the photographer, "is from *our* Georgia, in the States."

The photographer grinned. "Us Georgians got to stick together," he said, in a slow Atlanta drawl.

The Clown looked interested. "I have heard of such a place. But it is not like my Georgia, I suppose."

"I don't believe so," the photographer said. "But it's a mighty nice place."

"I would like to see it some day," the Clown said politely. He sat down in a big leather chair, crossing his long legs and looking a little more at ease.

The reporter had his notebook in his hand but it was inconspicuous, and when he took notes one was hardly aware of it. "That's an amazing story," he said to Liza, "a youngster like you bringing in a man from the Soviet Union on a borrowed passport."

"Not exactly borrowed," she said. "More like stolen."

Walter interrupted her quickly. "Don't say that, Liza. Your aunt gave you your uncle's passport, didn't she?"

"Yes, but that was because he loses things. She didn't intend me to use it for someone else." She wanted to be quite sure not to implicate Uncle George or Aunt May in any way.

"We understand that," the reporter said. He chuckled. "Uncle George must have been kind of startled at all he lost. You, sir," he said to the Clown, "I understand you had some problem with the KGB. Would you tell us about it?"

Slowly, painfully, the Clown answered his questions, looking often at Liza for help. She found that it was easy to skim over the details of the escape. The reporter was more interested in how they both felt, whether they had been frightened, how the Clown responded to his new freedom, and so on. He didn't press for details about the KGB's pursuit, but he was interested in the Clown's feelings about the Russian circus and his emotion at being cut off from his homeland. Liza thought the line of his questioning had echoes of the Solzhenitsyn affair, and if that was what he wanted, he got it. The Clown was visibly distressed when he spoke of never seeing Georgia again.

The photographer took some pictures while the interview was going on, and afterward he posed Liza and the Clown and a group including Harriet and Walter. The reporter thanked them profusely and at last the ordeal was over.

When the two men had gone, the Clown leaned his head back and closed his eyes. He looked pale and tense again. It upset Liza. They had had such a lovely day until all that happened.

Walter brought him some cognac, and Harriet made tea for all of them. "Don't worry," Walter said to the Clown. "I think things are going well."

"It's a terrible wrench for anybody," Harriet said, "leaving home."

Liza looked at her, and for the first time it occurred to her that leaving their own home and spending the last six years looking after her father and herself must have been a real sacrifice for Harriet and Walter. She was glad that after next year they would all go back, and Harriet and Walter would have the house to fix up. They would love that. But it kept on worrying her that she had been too self-concerned to realize how Harriet and Walter felt, even though she was so close to them. Aloud she said, "Children are horrible."

They all looked surprised and Harriet laughed. "That takes a prize for the remark-that-doesn't-follow-anything."

"In my head it follows," Liza said, but she didn't explain.

That evening after dinner Walter put some records on the stereo. Some of them were Liza's Dixieland albums, with Pete Fountain, George Lewis, and Papa

Celestin. She tried to explain to the Clown why she loved Dixieland, but it was hard to put into words.

"She's an anachronism," Harriet said. "Nobody plays Dixieland anymore except old-timers."

"Yes, there's a new thing about them," Walter said. "What is the bunch that goes around to colleges and packs 'em in? The Preservation Hall Band or something."

"Everything goes in cycles," Liza said. She had read that somewhere, and she liked the idea.

Harriet got Walter to jitterbug with her, although he protested that you couldn't jitterbug to Dixieland. They were very good, and Liza watched the Clown as he enjoyed them. She knew they were putting on a show to cheer him up, and she was grateful. It seemed to be working.

After awhile she persuaded him to try juggling some small individual silver salt cellars, which were the only things she could find that might do. They weren't precisely balanced, and the juggling wasn't his usual success but he tried. And doing it at all perked him up. She wished he had been able to bring all his props with him.

Later in the evening when the mood was quieter, Walter put on a record that had been one of Liza's father's favorites, a live recording of Marlene Dietrich's London concert. He showed the Clown the glamorous, young-looking picture of Dietrich on the album sleeve. "The lady is a grandmother," he told him. "She made her first big movie back in the Twenties—wasn't it the Twenties, Harriet?"

"I think so."

The Clown listened attentively, and Liza sat with her eyes closed on the divan. The album reminded her so much of her father. It was funny how vividly music could bring memories alive.

The Clown liked it. "It is astonishing, that voice," he said. "It is not really a good voice, hardly a singing voice at all, and yet it is magic." He asked to have "I Wish You Love" played again. He listened with a gentle smile as Dietrich introduced it by saying, "I sing it as a love song sung for a child."

Harriet, who was sitting beside Liza, knitting a scarf for Walter, sang the lyrics softly under her breath.

> *My breaking heart and I agree*
> *That you and I could never be,*
> *So with my best, my very best,*
> *I set you free.*
> *I wish you shelter from the storm,*
> *A cozy fire to keep you warm;*
> *But most of all, when snowflakes fall,*
> *I wish you love.*

The telephone rang, startling them. The Clown's expression of pleasure vanished.

Liza looked at her watch. "Uncle George should be on his way."

They all listened as Walter went into the library to answer it. He came out in a minute. "It's for you, Liza." He made a face. "Aunt May. And she's furious."

"Oh, dear." Liza took a long breath and went to cope with Aunt May.

Aunt May launched into her speech without preliminaries. "I don't know what you thought you were doing, Liza, leaving your uncle stranded like that, but it was a dirty rotten trick, especially after he was nice enough to look after you." She didn't wait for Liza's reply. "He is naturally completely bewildered . . . who wouldn't be? And it was a very disagreeable situation for him. If he hadn't happened to find a nice girl at the embassy to help him out, I don't know *what* . . ."

"Is he on his way home?" Liza finally managed to ask.

"Yes. He'll catch the plane for Kennedy right after the Moscow plane gets in, if it isn't late. Now Liza, I want you to check out there and make sure he makes it. If his plane is late, you'll just have to go get him and make arrangements. Do you understand?"

"Yes. Of course. I will. I'm sorry, Aunt May, it's too long to tell you now, but I'll write."

"I should think so. Some explanation. I can't go on talking at these outrageous rates, but really, Liza . . . You be sure and take care of him now, if necessary."

"Yes, I will. Don't worry."

"Very well." Aunt May hung up without saying good-bye.

"How did it go?" Harriet asked when she came back to the living room.

"Whew!" Liza said.

"I can imagine. Did you get a chance to explain?"

"Oh, heavens, no. You don't explain to Aunt May on overseas telephone." She took off her watch and put it on the table. "Uncle George is on the plane for Copenhagen now . . ."

"Oh, that is good!" the Clown said.

"I've got to check and see if he makes the connection for Kennedy. If not, we'll have a guest."

Walter went back to the library and called the airport to see if the Aeroflot plane was on schedule so far. "All's well," he said. "Liza, I'll stay up. You go to bed. You're tired."

"No, I wouldn't be able to sleep, thanks, Walter."

"We'll all sit up with you," Harriet said. "Unless you want to go to bed, Grigol."

The Clown said he would stay up, too.

Walter put more records on the stereo and lit a small fire in the fireplace. The Clown did card tricks for them. And finally they just sat and talked, the Clown telling them about his home and his work in the circus, Walter and Harriet talking about the American South. Liza listened sleepily and sipped the good Danish coffee that Harriet made.

At last it was time to call the airline. They all waited anxiously while Walter made the call. He came back smiling.

"All okay. The plane came in on time and good old Uncle George is now en route to New York."

"What a relief," Liza said. "Did they say whether he picked up his passport and things?"

"Yes, he did. Everything's copacetic."

"I too am much relieve," the Clown said. "That poor man, he has worry me very much."

"He'll have stories to tell the fellows back home for the next ten years," Harriet said. " 'The time I was stranded in Moscow.' "

"See?" Liza said to the Clown as they went upstairs.

"Everything's turning out lovely."

"Because of you," he said.

She had to look away because she knew her eyes were shining. She was so happy and things were going so beautifully.

14

On the same day that the Clown got his temporary Danish visa, Walter brought home several copies of the *International Herald Tribune,* with the story of Liza and the Clown under the caption, LATE U.S. CONSUL'S DAUGHTER SMUGGLES CLOWN OUT OF MOSCOW. There was a picture of Liza and the Clown in the living room of the flat.

The Clown listened anxiously while Liza read him the story. It was a condensed version of what Liza and the Clown had told the reporter, except that he had added the information about Liza's father. And he also said, "The Soviet authorities questioned George Asher closely, but they were satisfied that his was the role of the innocent bystander. Mr. Asher left Moscow twenty-four hours after his scheduled departure." He referred to the Clown as the "comic genius of the Georgian circus." The Clown shook his head in disapproval at that.

"There are no 'geniuses,'" he said. "We were a troupe."

"Never mind," Liza said. "I think you're a genius. And it's a nice story, isn't it? He didn't say anything wild. Except I wish he had left it out about Dad."

"You are your father's daughter," Harriet said. "You will be known for a long time as John Parke's daughter."

"I don't mean it that way," Liza said. "I love being known as his daughter. I just meant . . ."

Harriet gave her a little hug. "I know what you meant, sweetie."

"What I would like to suggest," Walter said, "is that we all go to the circus tonight." He looked at the Clown. "I hope you'll all agree, because I've already got the tickets."

The Clown seemed torn between pleasure at the idea of going to the circus and anxiety about being seen in public now that his identity and whereabouts were clearly established.

"I really think you're safer now that attention has been called," Walter said. "And you can't stay cooped up in the house."

"Don't push him, Walter," Harriet said. "It's his decision."

The Clown got up and walked restlessly up and down the room. "I'll go," he said at last. "It does frighten me, but as you say, not forever can I stay here."

"I didn't mean 'here,'" Walter said. "As far as any of

us are concerned, you're welcome here. I meant indoors, anywhere, hiding."

"I understand. I am very grateful. But I must think soon what I am to do. With no money, in a strange country, it is difficult to know."

In the afternoon the Copenhagen papers carried the story of the Clown.

That evening in their front row seats at the circus, he seemed to forget his anxieties. His expressive face showed his delight with the excellent circus acts. Late in the evening one of the clowns made a short speech in Danish.

Liza thought she must have misunderstood him. Her Danish was very shaky. And yet she heard. . . . She looked at Walter. "He didn't say what I thought he said?"

The crowd was clapping. A light swept slowly along the front row on their side.

"I hope he doesn't mind," Walter said.

"Grigol . . ." Liza began, but she was too late. The light came to rest on the Clown as the Danish clown in the ring called out in Danish and in English: "The great, brave Russian clown, Grigol Vakhtang!"

For a moment the Clown shrank back in alarm, but Liza caught his arm. "It's all right, Grigol. Walter told them."

The applause was tremendous. The Clown stood up and bowed, and the band began to play. The clapping increased. The Clown bowed and bowed, and the tears streamed down his face. Each time he sat down, the applause brought him to his feet again. The crowd wouldn't let him go. Someone shouted "Bravo!" and the voices all over the auditorium took it up. Walter had a broad grin on his face and Harriet was crying happily. Liza felt stunned.

Then the Clown reached for Liza's hand and pulled her to her feet. The applause sounded in her ears like thunder. It was frightening and wonderful at the same time. She didn't know what to do. She heard Harriet saying, "Smile at them, darlin'," so she managed a tremulous smile and sat down as soon as she could.

The Danish clown held out his hand to the Clown and led him into the arena. He handed him a collapsible opera hat. Liza gasped: how had he known? But then she remembered the Clown had told Walter and Harriet a little about his act.

The Clown popped open the hat, acting as if it had frightened him. The crowd roared with delight. No matter what he does tonight, Liza thought, they are going to love him. She felt warm all over with happiness. She reached over and squeezed Walter's hand.

With the hat and the arena, the Clown became a clown, no longer a worried young man on the run. He capered about as if he had suddenly been released from long captivity. He improvised all sorts of little comic touches with the other clown, almost as if they had worked together many times before. He did a long series of cartwheels and somersaults and leaps into the air as if he were on springs. The Danish clown ran to the side of the ring and came back with a big sketchpad and an enormous pencil. The Clown played a little scene of bashful rejection before he finally seized the pad and with his fast, sure strokes, sketched the Danish clown. He held it up and the crowd thundered its approval. He presented it to the clown with an elaborate bow and a sweep of his opera hat. Then he faced the crowd, flinging his arms wide as if to embrace them all, and he ran out of the ring and back to his seat, breathing quickly, smiling all over his face. He had to take half a dozen bows before the crowd would let him alone and the next act could proceed.

The Clown sat with his arm around Liza, watching in rapt pleasure as the circus finished. When it was over, people swarmed around to shake his hand and to praise Liza for her courage. She was breathless; nothing like this had ever happened to her in her life. All this wonderful acceptance for her Clown!

"Isn't he wonderful," she said to Harriet.

Harriet nodded. "He is."

"Walter, how did you ever think of telling them?"

"It just came to me while I was buying the tickets. I hunted up the Danish clown. He was very nice. They'd read the story."

"Oh, it was so wonderful."

A photographer had lured the Clown back into the ring for some pictures, and some of the other performers had come back in to meet him and talk to him. Liza and Harriet and Walter waited for him. The photographer wanted a picture of Liza, too, but she talked him out of it. This was the Clown's evening.

Now surely the offer would come from the Copenhagen Circus. Come and be our star clown. Maybe tonight it would come, or surely in the morning.

But it didn't come. Three days later it had still not come. The Clown pretended not to expect it. Walter said they had a budget; if there was no opening, there was no opening. Harriet said be patient. But Liza was bitterly disappointed. She wrote to Mademoiselle to ask her if she knew any of the people connected with the circus in Zurich, if there was a circus in Zurich. She told her briefly what had happened and how happy she was with her new friend. "But I must find him a job. He is restless and worried. He is my responsibility." She didn't say 'and I can't get along without him.'

On the morning of the fourth day she woke late. She heard Walter doing something or other out in the hall and singing, "Oh, Mr. Tambourine Man, play your song for me." He sounded happy.

When she came downstairs, the Clown was nowhere about.

"Where is he?" she asked Harriet.

"Doing a TV interview," she said. "Our celebrity."

"Oh, I forgot about that," Liza said. How could she have forgotten? She had promised to drive him to the studio.

"It's all right," Harriet said. "Walter took him."

"I'll go get him then. When is he through?"

"He's through by now. He had to go to the American Embassy."

"*American* Embassy. What for?"

"I don't know. He didn't know. He got a phone call to come over."

"How peculiar." Liza sat down and drank her juice while Harriet brought her some fresh-baked coffee cake.

"You have a letter from your aunt."

"Oh, jolly." Liza felt cross without knowing quite why. She finished her breakfast before she opened Aunt May's letter. When she had read it, she burst out laughing. "Harriet, listen to this. 'Dear Liza: just a note to let you know all is well with us. We had a reading of the will yesterday, and my dear father left me a remarkably generous inheritance, which of course doesn't compensate for his loss . . .'" Liza made a face. "'You will be glad to know that your uncle is basking in glory. He's quite the hero around here, for his part in helping rescue the Russian. Of course we understand now why you couldn't let him in on the plan. It would have been very dangerous for him if he had had the least inkling, when the Russians grilled him afterward. And they really did grill him. Only his total innocence, which was obvious even to them, saved him.'"

Harriet laughed. "Where ignorance is bliss, 'tis folly to be wise."

"'The story of the escape hit all the papers here, with a lovely picture of you, and it was on the TV news as well. Remember us to the Russian. Keep well and write soon. Love, *Aunt May*.'" Liza put the letter down and shook her head. "You never know, do you?"

"I told you, love, you worry about too many things." Harriet poured herself a cup of coffee. "I suppose Grigol will be leaving us soon."

Liza looked up, startled. "He hasn't had an offer, has he?"

"No, but he's bound to get one somewhere, with all the lovely publicity. And he's such a beautiful clown. We have to be prepared for it, don't we?"

"I don't see why," Liza said. "He's sure to get an offer here, and he can simply stay on as he is now. We're all happy, aren't we?"

"Liza . . ." Harriet said. Then she shook her head.

"Don't try to hang on."

Liza felt her face stiffen. "I don't know what you mean."

"I just don't want you to break your heart."

Liza put down her napkin and got up. "Honestly, Harriet," she said, "sometimes you make no sense."

"All right," Harriet said softly. "All right."

15

The hours went by and the Clown still hadn't come back. Liza kept looking out the window. "Maybe he's lost," she said.

"He can take a taxi."

"Maybe he's forgotten the address."

"No, honey, he has it in his pocket, and anyway he knows it by heart. Don't fret so. He's a grown man."

"Anything could happen," Liza said. "He could get hit by a car. The Russians could have found him . . ."

Harriet moved around her with a dustcloth. "Move, honey."

"He could be in mortal danger, and we stand here talking."

Harriet stopped dusting to look at her. "We're all in

mortal danger every minute of the day, if you want to start brooding about that." Then, more gently, she said, "He's all right, Liza. You've just gotten used to being responsible for him. But he's all right now; you can turn him loose."

"I'm going for a walk," Liza said abruptly.

"Good idea. It's a nice day."

Liza got a sweater and put on her beret with the unstitched lining. "Turn him loose." Harriet made him sound like a colt or something.

She walked through a maze of narrow streets in the general direction of the Frederiksholms Canal, and stopped on the bridge near the Christiansborg Palace. Tourists with cameras were strolling across the big cobblestone courtyard of the palace. She leaned on the stone bridge and looked down at the colorful launches tied up along the side. A big launch full of tourists moved slowly along the canal. She thought of the first time she and her father had come to Copenhagen and had taken that little trip. A photographer had snapped a picture of them which she still had. It had been a particularly happy time, and now it seemed so long ago.

She leaned down and stared at the slowly moving water. There ought to be some way a person could hang on to happiness when it came. Instead, it was always just slipping away, even while you were enjoying it. It was pulled right out from under your feet, and the present kept turning into the future. Like the water in the river, she thought, it won't stay put. If she were fond of sloppy metaphors, she could write a whole paper that Miss Anhalt would absolutely love, for English class, on the analogy between life and a river. Of time and the river. Well, yes, someone else seemed to have thought of it already. And what was that old thing by Thoreau that she'd always thought of as folksy and woodsy and not making much sense . . . "Time is a river I go a-fishing in," or something to that effect. It suddenly struck her as possibly true, except you couldn't fish just anywhere. She didn't like it.

She would have liked to stop time, at least for a longish stay, during that half hour or so at the circus when she and the Clown had stood up together and were applauded. Even the scary journey had been very beautiful in a way. They had been so close, so dependent on each other. And now everybody else claimed him, and Harriet was saying things like: "let him be," "don't hang on." Harriet hung on to Walter, though, if anybody cared to notice. Oh, the whole business was impossible. How could anybody be expected to deal with life in a reasonable, logical way, when it was itself so unreasonable?

Impatiently she turned away from the canal and wandered aimlessly. After awhile she came to the fountain on Gammeltorv. She had been there during the Easter holidays last year, on the queen's birthday, to see the traditional golden apples, the little gold metal balls that danced on the water jets of the fountain. The golden apples made her think of the Clown's silver juggling balls, and she set out to find a magic shop or someplace where she could get him some new ones. She wandered all through the maze of pedestrian streets called Strøget until at last she saw a little shop advertising TRICKS, JOKES, MAGIC, tucked away almost out of sight.

It was a very crowded little shop, and at first she

couldn't even see the proprietor, but he bobbed up at last, looking like a character from Hans Christian Andersen. It took some doing to make him understand what she wanted. He spoke no English, and she didn't know the Danish words she needed. Finally she drew a picture of half a dozen balls at different heights and then pantomimed juggling. At last he understood. He didn't have any silver balls, but he had golden ones. She bought a dozen. If the Clown didn't want them, she could always donate them to the queen's birthday, she thought, smiling to herself and feeling much better.

She stopped at the open air fruit and vegetable market and bought some peaches and pears for Harriet. She had been cross with Harriet, and she was sorry. It wasn't Harriet's fault that life didn't always come to heel when Liza gave the command. As she was about to leave the market, she saw some huge strawberries that Walter would love. In the end she was so laden with packages she had to take a taxi home.

Surely the Clown would be back by now. She could not imagine what the American Embassy had wanted him for. If she'd known he was going there, she could have taken him up and introduced him. She knew most of the staff. Oh, well. As Harriet would say, he undoubtedly survived on his own.

She let herself into the flat, almost dropping the peaches. "Hey, help!" she called. "I come bearing gifts."

They were in the kitchen, all three of them, and they looked at her with such strange, bemused faces she had a sense of watching a play. They were sitting on the bar stools and, of all things, they were drinking champagne.

"Champagne?" she said. "In the middle of the afternoon?"

Walter jumped up, at last, to take her packages. "Hey, strawberries," he said. "Bigger than cannonballs. Peaches. Pears."

"What's up?" Liza was looking at the Clown. His face was radiant. It came to her suddenly that he'd gotten a job with the circus. "You got a job!" she said. "You did, didn't you? The circus people called you!" She'd been wrong after all; you *could* hang on to happiness, at least for a while. "You did get a job?"

The Clown put down his glass. "The most wonderful job."

"Oh, I knew you would."

"Liza," Harriet said.

But Liza was too excited and happy to stop talking. "And now you can stay here, and we'll all be happy. And look what I brought you." She gave him the package of golden balls.

He looked so moved, she thought he was going to cry. But he jumped suddenly to his feet and began juggling the balls. First two, then three, then four. Five, six. Six golden apples flying through the air with such dazzling speed they became almost a single flow of gold to the eye. Seven, eight. They all watched him, laughing and excited. The balls made a golden halo over his head. Then at last he dropped one.

"Oh, my!" Harriet said. "Wasn't that pretty!"

Liza settled happily on a stool. "Can I have some champagne? When does the job start? Are they giving you a decent salary? The cost of living is high in Copenhagen so don't let them get you cheap."

"Liza . . ." Harriet said again.

Walter poured half a glass of champagne for Liza, and she sipped it. It was good. In less than three weeks she would be seventeen. Always on her birthday she had been allowed to do something that she had previously been too young to do. Like riding a new two-wheeled bike when she was six. And learning to drive when she was fifteen.

"I think when I'm seventeen," she said, "I'll have a small champagne party. You can pop the cork," she said to the Clown, "and Walter will pour."

"Liza, listen to Grigol's news," Harriet said. "About his job."

"Well, I'm trying to listen. Nobody's telling me." She smiled at him. "Tell me about it."

He took a deep breath. "It's in America."

Liza put her glass down very carefully. It was one of the Waterford glasses she'd given Harriet for Christmas. It wouldn't do to drop it. "What?"

"He got this fantastic offer from Ringling," Walter said, talking faster than usual. "They cabled the U.S. Embassy to find him. Huge salary, plane fare, an advance, you name it."

"And my own act," the Clown said. His eyes shone. "I can do my own act."

Harriet put her hand on Liza's shoulder. "Isn't that great, honey? He's going to have a tremendous career."

Liza felt choked and the muscles in her face didn't work right when she tried to smile. "Yes, I . . . It's marvelous," she said. "It's fantastic, isn't it. Ringling."

"And when you all come to America," the Clown said, "we will have such fine times. You will show me Georgia, U.S.A. Yes?"

"Yes. Fine." It's only fifteen months till we go to America, Liza thought. Fifteen months. I'll be eighteen. The Clown will be a great American success, probably

179

a movie star too, like Marcel Marceau. He won't re-member my name. "I hope you'll have a wonderful success," she said.

The Clown took her by the shoulders and looked at her with those dark, soulful, Georgian eyes. "And it is all because of you. You give me a new life."

She broke away from him and ran upstairs.

Through her closed doors she could hear the murmur of their voices from time to time and then the closing of the front door. After a while there was a knock. At first she thought she would pretend to be asleep. She had been crying and didn't want to talk to anyone. But the knock came again.

"Yes?"

"It's me," Harriet said. "I'm coming in, if you don't mind." She pushed the door open and brought in a tray with sandwiches and a glass of milk and a peach. "Thought you might be hungry."

"Thank you." Liza turned her face away, but she knew there was no hiding anything from Harriet. There never had been.

"Walter's taken him out to get him some clothes and to go to the bank and all that. And pick up the plane ticket. They'll be gone awhile. Would you like those ducks for dinner?"

"Yes. I don't care."

Harriet sat down on the food of the bed. "We've got to be happy for him. It sounds like a wonderful chance."

"I know."

There was a long pause. Liza wished Harriet would go away.

"Things work out funny, don't they," Harriet said. "Funnier than you think they will, even. Like if anybody had told me when I first got married that I'd end up in Europe looking after Johnny Parke's young 'un . . ."

Liza turned to look at her. "Do you hate it?"

"Hate it! How you talk. Of course I don't hate it. It's been great."

"You get homesick."

"Sure I get homesick. That doesn't say I'd want to give up all I've had. Not by a country mile." She gave Liza a gentle pat. "Sometimes we get the bitter with the sweet. That's life, I guess."

"When is he leaving?"

"The day after tomorrow, I think it's nine something in the morning."

Liza gasped. "So soon!"

"They wanted him right away. And it's just as well, honey. I mean why prolong the agony?"

"What agony?" Liza's voice was harsh. "Who's agonizing?"

"We'll all miss him."

"People come, and people go. All you have to remember is not to get involved with them."

"That would be a pretty drab life."

Liza flared up. "It would make a lot more sense. You love somebody, and right away you lose them. I'm never going to love anybody again."

"Don't say that," Harriet said sternly. "I know you're upset, but don't you talk like that, Liza Parke. That's cowardly."

"It's all very well for you to talk," Liza said. Her heart beat so hard it made her chest hurt. "You've never been through it."

"What do you know about what I've been through?"

Harriet stood up. She looked angry. "What makes you think you're the only one in the world who suffers?"

"That's not fair. I never said that."

"But you think so. All right, you've had your trials. I'm the last one to say you haven't. But you're not the whole show. Anybody who feels anything suffers. You love and you lose and you lose and you think it's nothing but pain and loss . . ."

"That's what I'm saying. So don't love people."

Harriet gave her a long look. "Then you might as well be dead." She went out of the room.

Liza lay down without eating. After a long time she fell asleep and dreamed for the first time in a long time about the man with no face.

16

Liza got through dinner, but she knew her manner was puzzling the Clown. She was so afraid of bursting into tears every time anyone spoke to her that she defended herself with a cool, slightly mocking manner. She disparaged America, making them laugh with her descriptions of hamburger heavens and neon horrors, but the laughter was uneasy because each in his own way knew she was fighting to keep her self-control. Only Harriet wholly understood what was wrong.

Liza excused herself as early as she could, with the plea of being tired.

The next day the Clown was gone almost all day, attending to the last-minute details, buying luggage, picking up a suit that had had to be altered, getting his

American visa, and so on. In the evening he took them all out to dinner at the Fiskehuset, and afterward they walked in Tivoli Gardens and listened to some of the bands. It should have been a memorable evening, but Liza's heart was heavy and all she could think of was getting home to her room so she wouldn't have to keep up her end of the conversation.

In the mailbox when they got home she found another letter from Aunt May. She read it aloud to them. " 'Dear Liza: It's me again. We were talking about that sketch the Russian Clown made of your Uncle George. I threw it away in Moscow because your uncle didn't care for it, but we've had second thoughts since all that's happened. It would be fun to have it framed and hang it over the fireplace. It would make such a nice conversation piece. Would you ask him if he'd do another? I'm enclosing a snapshot in case he doesn't remember what Uncle George looks like . . .' "

The Clown laughed.

" '. . . and of course we would pay him. Would you think ten dollars would be satisfactory? You sound him out and let us know. Yours with love and haste, *Aunt May.*' "

"Oh, wow," Walter said. "They are really too much, aren't they?"

"Ten dollars," Harriet said. "Lady Bountiful."

"I'll tell her you're too busy," Liza said.

"No, no," the Clown said. "I will do one, of course. Before I leave, if you will please send it to her with my compliments. After all, this Uncle George did much for me."

"But not exactly on purpose," Harriet said.

"All the same."

As soon as I don't see him anymore, Liza thought, as they all said good night to each other, it will be easy. Just put him right out of my mind.

"I'll call you at seven," Harriet said to her. "We'll have a good breakfast and leave at eight."

Liza was standing on the third step of the stairs that led to the bedrooms. The Clown was just below her and Walter and Harriet were putting out lights and tidying up. "I'm not going to the airport," Liza said. The look of hurt in the Clown's eyes came and went so quickly, she thought she had imagined it.

"Of course," he said. "It is far too early."

"Not go?" Harriet was looking at her, a half plumped-up sofa cushion in her hands.

"I hate good-byes in airports and railroad stations." Liza knew her voice sounded strange. I sound brittle and bright, she thought, like an old Bette Davis movie. Life is an old Bette Davis movie. How's that for an English paper? How's that, Miss Anhalt, love? She held out her hand to the Clown. "You're going to have a smashing career. Best of luck." Her hand was cool and steady. Miss Liza Parke was back in the saddle again.

He took the cue. Hs own voice was quiet and gentle, but he kept his usual Georgian emotion out of it. "I can never thank you enough, Liza."

"No need." She retrieved her hand and started up the stairs.

She knew he was standing there looking up at her, but she didn't look back. No use to push her luck. She closed her bedroom door firmly, and went quickly to bed. She heard the Copenhagen bells strike midnight and play the little silvery tune. She heard them strike one and two but not three.

She woke early and heard the morning sounds of footsteps and running water and the faint clink of dishes. She smelled the coffee and the bacon. She was very hungry. As soon as they were gone, she would go downstairs and eat a big breakfast and then . . . Then what? She would have to think of something very interesting to do. A project for the summer. How about studying Greek? Everybody said nobody learned Greek any more, so it might be a fun thing to do.

After half an hour or so, she heard the Clown come upstairs and presumably get his luggage. There was the faint thump of suitcases. Then his receding footsteps and soon the closing of the front door. She heard Walter start up the Mini and rev it the way he always did. She heard him back it out of the parking area. She lay very still for a few minutes, clasping her hands tightly together. She felt cold.

When she got out of bed, she saw a piece of paper under her door. The sketch of Uncle George, she thought. She opened the door. Yes, there was the sketch, signed in careful Roman letters, "To Mr. George Asher, with best wishes, Grigol Vakhtang." It was quite good. But there was another sketch under it. She picked it up. It was a sketch of the Clown himself. It showed him in his top hat and his huge spectacles, the red spots on his cheeks. It was a head and shoulders sketch. His head was tilted back, his mouth in a round *O* of surprise, one eyebrow cocked. He was looking at a series of little golden balls that were flying around his head. He had signed the sketch: "For Liza—I wish you love—Grigol."

Liza burst into tears. But after a minute she pulled herself together and got dressed faster than she had ever dressed before. She flew down the stairs, grabbed her purse, and ran down the three flights of stairs to the lobby. Heedless of traffic she ran out into the street looking for a taxi. Within minutes she was on her way to the airport.

She didn't know the gate number, but when she told the driver it was SAS for New York, he got her to the right end of the terminal. When she found them, the Clown was just going through the electronic checkpoint. Walter and Harriet were watching him from the non-passenger side.

"Grigol!" She dashed past the guard and threw her arms around the Clown. His face changed from surprise to delight. He hugged her tightly while the guard fussed.

"Liza. I'm so glad you came."

"I'm a selfish beast. I was sulking. But Grigol, I do love you dearly, and I do want you to have a wonderful life . . . I mean it. And when we come to America to live, we'll have marvelous times . . ." She was crying.

"Dear Liza, dear Liza, don't cry. It will be fine. It will all be splendid. We will never forget one moment, eh?"

"Please," the guard was saying plaintively, "Mademoiselle, if you please . . ."

"I'm sorry." Liza released the Clown and moved back to the proper side of the line. "Be careful," she said to the Clown. "Don't get run over. Write often."

The sepulchral voice of the loudspeaker announced in Danish, Swedish, and English the departure time of the plane. "All passengers will please board at once."

She watched his tall figure until he was out of sight. Then she turned back to Walter and Harriet. Harriet hugged her. "I like you," Harriet said. "I like you, Liza Parke."

"Well, let's go home," Liza said. "I'm hungry. I think I'm going to learn Greek this summer."

Temple Israel

Minneapolis, Minnesota

In Honor of the Bar Mitzvah of

MICHAEL MARK

By His Parents,

DR. & MRS. AARON MARK

June 4, 1977